THIRD TIME'S A CHARM

HEATHER MORRIS

ISBN: 1497354420
ISBN-13: 978-1497354425

DEDICATION

This book is dedicated to my husband and girls who don't see me much when I'm in the writing mode. Thank you for insisting I write my own stories and for allowing me the time and space to do so.

THE COLVIN SERIES BOOK LIST
(SO FAR)

Book 1- Down to the Creek – Aiden & Karlie

Book 2- Nursery in Bloom – Austin & Leah

Book 3- Third Time's a Charm – Audrey & Maysen

ACKNOWLEDGMENTS

I would like to thank my Aunt Sandra Jones for painting the cover painting for me. She took my ideas and made something wonderful!

I would also like to thank those who are so excited and willing to read my stories for me before I take the next step with them. It means the world to me that my family and friends are so supportive of this hobby. Their encouragement keeps the stories coming with every book.

Lastly, I would like to thank those who have bought my books and helped to give me the willpower to continue on. Without your support I couldn't keep writing and publishing them.

1

"You mean to tell me you had your Prince Charming sitting across from you and you didn't get his number? How do you plan on ever seeing this handsome creature again? Audrey have I not taught you anything?" I hear Karlie say to me from across the room.

We're all together this afternoon in New York getting dressed up and makeup done for the Shannon's Crusade Benefit tonight. Leah and my brother Austin helped to set up a charity to help battered women much like Leah before she came to Colvin. The charity helps women to get out of those relationships and to find a safe place to live. It's an amazing thing they're doing and our whole family is so proud of what they've accomplished and continue to do for the cause.

"Karlie, how was I supposed to ask a strange man I just met for his number? Wouldn't that be awkward?"

"Have you tried to find him at all since you got back home? It's been a month Audrey." Leah says while looking at me in the reflection of the mirror she's watching the hairdresser do her hair in. Aiden and Austin surprised us with the hairdresser and makeup artist for the night's festivities. Of course we all squealed like little girls.

"No, I haven't tried. I was too scared I wouldn't find him."

3

"Or would find him.   What did you say his name was, Maysen Correli, right? I'm going to look him up online while I wait for Leah to get done."

"Karlie, no. I don't think that's a good idea. He didn't give me his number or ask for mine either remember?" I say trying to keep them from butting in any more than they already have. In our family matchmaking comes naturally whether we like it or not.

"Too late, I can't find anything under that name anyway. Nothing on social media either."

"Social media? Aiden would be horrified to know you were associated with social media."

"I know we've been butting heads about using it to spread the word even more about the breeding program. He's against it but I think it would be a smart idea. Leah uses it for Shannon's Crusade and its done great, right Leah?"

"Yes, actually it's been a great marketing tool for us. However that doesn't mean it's a solution for you guys."

"But don't you think Aiden should at least try it before turning it down? I tried getting him to look at it with me but he tells me he's too busy. He's being a pain with the whole thing. Doesn't want the world in the middle of what's going on."

"Well, after what I went through with the media, I don't blame him. You have to learn how to control the interest and the invasion of your privacy. I don't think Aiden will ever be ready for that."

"Maybe you're onto something. I guess I've been the stubborn one. I better go call my husband and apologize. I'll be right back." Karlie takes her phone and heads for the bathroom leaving Leah and I alone looking at each other through the mirror again.

"You're welcome for turning that around and getting the heat off of you and your mystery man."

"Leah, I really don't think I can look for him. I think it's just too weird. It wasn't meant to be so it didn't happen."

"You really believe that Audrey?"

"Actually I think we were meant to meet to make me realize I really do want a family and I do want my happily ever after like you two have."

"Audrey you will have yours when God intends on it. It's all mapped out for you. You do believe that don't you?"

"Yes, I do I'm just getting impatient." I smile and start getting my dress and panty hose on. "I know it'll happen someday I just got a little excited when I met someone new and better, ya know?"

"I do. I never in a million years dreamed that moving to Colvin to escape the drama would turn into my happily ever after as you put it. I just followed my heart and here we are. Don't lose faith Aud."

"Thanks Leah, you're the best."

"The best? What about me? I knew you first!" I hear Karlie exclaim from the bathroom doorway. She's off the phone and standing there with a pout.

"One of the best. Is that better?" I walk and hug her before taking a deep breath and continue getting dolled up.

"So we concluded on no Prince Charming search huh? That's no fun. Maybe you'll meet another one tonight. They'll all have tuxes on and looking dashing."

"Karlie!" Leah and I both yell as she starts on another matchmaking rant. She looks up at us and smiles her sweet big smile we all love.

"Thanks but no thanks. I think I'll just go one day at a time. When it's time it'll happen." I shrug off the uneasy longing and take my turn in the hairdresser's chair.

"If you say so. Karlie and I will be here if you need us. Right Karlie?" Leah says and glares at Karlie making her point with that look.

"Yep. When you need us, we're always here. Now, let's finish so I can see MY Prince Charming in a tux again!"

****

Knock knock knock

"That would be the guys! Let's go knock their socks off!" Karlie squeals as she hears the knocks.

"Let's go. I'm just warning you there will be a lot of cameras and people. Are you sure you want to walk the red carpet with me? You can go straight in the back door if you want, Austin and I won't mind."

"I think I'll go in the back but you and Aiden should go with them if you want." I say and try to act like nothing's wrong with me. I really don't want to be in front of all the cameras and people right now. They might think I'm okay with not having a significant other but I'm really not. I ache to have that love and happiness. I think I could hear my biological clock ticking louder than my heart beat. I can't let everyone know how depressed I am about this. They would think they have to jump in and fix it. This isn't going to be an easy fix though. So I smile and pretend.

"Ok, see you in there." Karlie and Leah smile with so much excitement for what's to come tonight. But I'm sitting here envious of their lives.

2

"Dude, what is up with you? You've been weird since you came back from Tulsa. Is it your mom? Is she ok?" I hear Carter say next to me in the car.

"Ya she's good. I think she's going home soon. I'm just tired I guess. Lots going on in my head."

"She's coming home here or where?"

"She thinks she wants to go to her sister's in Colvin but I can't let her do that. But I can't get down there as often to check on her and she needs someone near."

"So you're thinking you need to go to Tulsa now too?"

"You know me well. Yes, I'm really debating on moving back to Tulsa so I can be the one to be there for Mom now. I wouldn't miss this place, that's for sure."

"Will your Mom adopt me?" Carter says and puts the car in park as we pull up at Rod's Garage. The place we call home during the day and far too many late nights working on other people's cars and knowing Rod charged them an arm and a leg. Always makes me feel like the sleaze he is and having to see the looks on the faces of our customers when they get the bill makes me sick.

"Did you see that hot blonde that came in yesterday right after lunch? She needed a jump but Rod took her in his Caddy and probably charged her a couple hundred dollars."

I panic and look at Carter. Hot blonde? Couldn't be Audrey. She lives in Tulsa. I tried to find her on the internet but couldn't find anyone with that name in Tulsa. I could have sworn she lived there, but if she does she isn't on any social media sites.

"Blonde? What did she look like?"

"Whoa dude, what's up with you? Seriously? You just went pale when I told you about the hottie. Did you know her or what?"

"No I don't think so. I didn't even see her."

"Uh huh. Let me get this straight. You have been acting like a spaz ever since you came back from Tulsa and you really don't have much to say about what happened while you were there. Now an unidentified blonde comes in the garage and you freak out."

"You're delusional."

"Who is she?"

"Who is who?"

"The chick that has you all up in arms."

"I don't know what you're talking about. Can we get to work? Rod will be here soon and if we're not working he'll fire us both."

"You're moving to Tulsa what do you care?"

"I'm not gone yet. I haven't made up my mind."

"Who is she? Come on Dude, I know there's a chick involved in this equation somewhere. And we're not talking your Mom."

"How do you know that? I didn't say a word about her." I say with a big sigh. I'm caught. Wonderful I didn't want to talk to Carter about Audrey. He'll really think I'm a coward when he finds out I didn't even get the girl's number.

"Dude it's all making sense now. No wonder you've been all weird and stuff since you got back. Spill it."

"Fine! But I don't want to hear your opinions when I'm done. Got it?"

"Deal." He smiles big and I should have known it wasn't real. He could never stay quiet about my love life. Or lack thereof.

"I was at the hospital one day visiting Mom and I took a detour past the nursery where I saw this woman standing outside the glass looking in like she was enchanted by all the babies inside. I asked if one was hers but she said her brother and sister in law had just had one and that she didn't have any kids of her own. We talked for a bit there and then had coffee together in the cafeteria. Her name was Audrey. She was blonde. That's all there is to say. I'll never see her again but I can't quit seeing her face everywhere."

"And when I said some blonde was here you thought she might have come to see you. Have you called her at all since you've been back? It's been like a month. Did she move to Africa or something or join a convent?"

"I didn't get her number. Just her name."

"Dude you have got to be kidding me!"

"I said no opinions remember?"

"That was before I knew you committed such a travesty against the male species! You always get hot girls' numbers! Dude

I'm ashamed!"

"I know, I know. I was so enamored by her that I forgot about that part until after she left. I could have kicked myself when I realized it. Believe me I feel like such a dumb ass!"

"Have you tried finding her online? You know her whole name don't ya?"

"I have looked yes, and nothing. No one by that name in Tulsa and only four hundred in the U.S. alone."

"You're screwed then!"

"Wow such a big supporter here. I know I screwed up but I can't get her out of my head."

"I don't think you have a choice. Is that another reason why you're thinking of moving back to Tulsa? Thinking you'll chance upon her again?"

"No. Maybe. I don't really know. I just haven't felt right since I came back here."

"You have it bad my friend and I don't see it ending any time soon."

"Great. Do you wanna move with me?"

"I'll have to consult my little black book and see if it would allow."

"You're a pig."

"Oink oink." And he walks away laughing while I shake my head. He is definitely a male pig when it comes to women. Me on the other hand, I'm a lot more reserved. Obviously. I didn't even get Audrey's phone number. Idiot.

****

We're starting a tow service for the garage and now I have to be the first one on call. Wonderful, another way for Rod to squeeze more money out of unsuspecting people. I have to take this dumb pager home with me tonight and hope no one calls it. A pager? Who uses a pager anymore? I grunt and throw it in the passenger side of the pickup as I get in and fire the engine.

"Hey Mom, how ya feeling?" I say after dialing her number. I haven't talked to her today and she was supposed to hear from the doctor about getting out of the hospital soon so I figure I had better check in.

"Hey honey. I'm doing well today. Doctor says he thinks I can get out of here by the end of next week. Isn't that great news?"

"Ma that's amazing news. I think I'm going to move back to Tulsa. Carter might come with me."

"Are you sure about that Maysen? I don't need you to come hover over me. I'm not a child."

"I know that Ma but I would feel so much better if I at least lived in the same town instead of a different state."

"I have to admit I would love to see you closer but that's your choice Son. Aunt Ingrid said she would come stay with me once I got out until I was able to be alone. You just let us know when you think you're coming if you decide."

"Ok Ma I'll let ya know. I'm thinking next week and that will give me a couple days to get my stuff in order here. I won't miss working at this crummy garage that's for sure."

"I know Rod isn't a very nice man. He doesn't know what good people he has working there for him. It will definitely be his loss."

"Alright Ma I'll let ya go. I just got home and need a shower pretty badly. I'll talk to you tomorrow. Love you."

"Love you too Son. Take care."

I hang up the phone and head straight to my shower. Carter and I share the rent on this two bedroom dump of a house but he's never really here. He's always staying out late with a different woman each night. I'm not sure his moving to Tulsa would be a good move for his social calendar. I chuckle knowing he's probably using that to his advantage right now. Pig.

****

"Dude, what time did you get in? I got home at 2am and you weren't here. Decide to tie one on before you head back to Oklahoma?"

"No Carter, I had a tow about midnight. You were supposed to go with me but since you were out partying again I had to do it alone. Thanks, by the way."

"Ah man I'm so sorry. I didn't realize it was our turn with that damned pager last night."

"Who else's turn would it be? No one else is going to do it but us. Rod isn't going to do it and Lou wouldn't do it because he would have to leave the bar long enough."

"I didn't think of that. This sucks. Are we going to always be on call now?"

"Probably. I've decided though that I'm giving Rod my notice in the morning. Not very good notice but who cares. Rod won't."

"You're really leaving huh?"

"Yep. Mom thinks she's going to get out end of next week so I need to be there by then."

"Ok man, I guess we both give our notices in the morning. I can't let you go alone. I can't let you have all the fun searching for Miss Right either. You are going to try to find her again once you're down there right?"

"I don't know Carter I'll be busy getting Mom situated and finding another job."

"Well, do you need a ride to work today or are you taking your bike?"

"Bike. I'll see you a little later. I need to run a few errands before I go in. Rod can like it or not. I really don't care."

"See ya at the office man." I watch the best friend I have had since moving to Omaha six years ago for college. Once I finished my automotive courses I was a certified mechanic and ready to start turning wrenches. I didn't know however how hard it was going to be to get a good job. I took the first one I found and happened to meet Carter who had also just started. We've been best buds since. And now we're moving to Tulsa together next week. Wild.

HEATHER MORRIS

3

"Audrey glad to see you're back. How was New York and the benefit?" I hear the principal of the school, Mrs. Simms, saying from behind me. I turn and see her standing in the doorway of my classroom and smiling. She's such a wonderful lady and I'm so blessed to have this job that I love. Right after I graduated college in Tulsa, I was granted this position because the current second grade teacher was leaving to have a baby and didn't want to come back. I have been here ever since then enjoying every student I have the pleasure of teaching. Seeing those little people come in one student and leave a completely different one at the end of the year is very gratifying. And I think I kinda rock as a teacher!

"The benefit was amazing. It was beautiful and raised so much money for Shannon's Crusade. Thank you for covering my classroom for me on Friday so that I could join the rest of my family. Not something I would want to do every day. But it was great to get away, even better to be back home. There were so many people snapping pictures everywhere you turned it was unreal."

"I can only imagine. Your kids were perfect angels like always. They missed you but will be glad to have you back today. Have a great day Miss Blake." She smiles and walks away.

"Oh I forgot the main reason I stopped by. There are a

bunch of new guidelines coming down from the higher ups and we need someone to go to Omaha to the conference they're holding to explain them."

"More guideline changes huh? Didn't we just get a slew of them at the beginning of the school year? It should be informative for whomever you send I'm sure. I look forward to getting the packet once they're back."

"Actually I would like you to go Audrey. You're so good at understanding and explaining these dumb changes that we would benefit most by having you there."

"Ok well, let me know when it is and I'll pencil it in."

"Um, you need to leave in the morning."

"The morning? I just got back from New York. I haven't even unpacked yet."

"I'm sorry this is such short notice but we just found out on Friday about the conference and actually the one in Omaha is the last one. We won't have another chance at one if you don't go tomorrow. I've already registered you and taken care of the rental car and hotel. You're all set."

"Great. I guess I'm off to Omaha for a few days. How long is the conference?"

"It's only on Wednesday. You fly up tomorrow and fly home on Thursday."

"Ok well I guess I'll see you Friday. I assume you've found a sub for my classroom?"

"Yes, it's all set. If you would prefer to go home today and get ready to leave I would be more than happy to cover your class today myself. I'll leave that up to you."

"I think leaving after lunch would be best. I have so much to get done before I leave again for another couple of days. Goodness nothing like short notice."

"Like I said, I'm very sorry about that. It really couldn't be helped."

"I'll see you after lunch then. Thank you."

"I'll send you an email of the itinerary and other details. Thanks again Audrey. I knew I could count on you."

"Of course." I smile as big as I can while my insides are churning. I really don't want to go on another trip let alone this soon. Goodness, this better be a good conference.

****

"Hi, my name is Audrey Blake and I'm here to pick up my rental car. It should be ready to go."

"Ah yes, Audrey Blake from Colvin School District in Colvin, Oklahoma am I correct?"

"Yes sir that's correct."

"Could I see your driver's license please? Ah thank you Miss Blake. Your car is in row 8 space C. Here are your keys and thank you for renting with us. Have a great trip."

"Thank you." I take the keys from the gentleman and walk towards the rows of cars. 1, 2, 3, 4, 5, 6, 7 and finally row 8. Seriously? They start with Z on this end? And he said C? Ugh!

After finally getting to the rental car and being able to sit down, I successfully follow the GPS lady's instructions and am headed down the right road towards my hotel. There sure is a lot more traffic here than I'm used to. This is crazy!

Seems like I've been driving for an hour when I feel the car stutter and slow down. I look at the speedometer and it shows the speed is gradually lowering and lowering. I don't see any lights on the dash either and that makes the hair on the back of my neck stand up. I don't know anything about cars or how they run. I just start it and put it in drive. I'm smart enough to know I need to pull over and get out of this gnarly traffic. I turn on my right blinker and slowly ease out of each lane and come to a stop along the shoulder.

I sit in the car and feel the vibrations of the cars that zoom by beside me. This cannot be happening. Weren't rental cars supposed to be reliable? But I suppose on the school's budget they went with the cheapest route meaning less reliable. Wonderful.

I try to start the car again but it just won't go. What am I supposed to do now? I fish my cell phone out of my purse and ask it to find the nearest cab company's phone number.

"Alex's Cabs 217-555-3333. Would you like me to dial this number for you?" I hear the phone reply.

"Yes." And it's ringing. "Yes, I need a cab. My rental car broke down alongside the highway leading from the airport to downtown Omaha. I'm really not sure where I am, but I see a sign for the Downtown Historical Museum. Does that help? Oh wonderful. It's a small black car. Thank you again." Fifteen minutes? I was hoping for five. Sitting alongside this road is kinda creepy so I dial Karlie's number hoping Aiden doesn't answer. He would throw a fit to know I'm stranded in a strange place like this.

"Aud where are you? I went by the ranch earlier but your Mom said you were out of town again? Where on Earth did you run off to?"

"Hey Karlie, I'm in Omaha, Nebraska right now for a conference tomorrow. I'll be home on Thursday. Well that is if I'm not murdered alongside this darn highway. My rental car broke down and the cab company said it would be like fifteen minutes before anyone could get here. So I sit."

"Alone? Oh my goodness Audrey that sounds so creepy!

I'll tell Aiden to call a garage near there and hopefully someone can get the car towed for you. We'll also make sure you get a new rental by morning. Don't worry we'll take care of you."

"That's not why I called you. I can take care of it myself. I'm going to get to the hotel and then call a tow company. Once they have it at the shop I'll call the rental place and see what they say. No big deal, I believe the conference is in the same hotel I'm staying in. Won't need a car until the drive back to the airport on Thursday."

"Ok well if you need us to do anything you let us know."

"Don't worry about me, I'm an adult remember? Well looks like the cab is here early. Gotta go. Love you. See you Thursday."

"Bye be safe!" I hear her say as I hit end and throw my phone back in the purse.

"Hi you're here sooner than expected. That's great news since it's kinda creepy sitting here alone. I need to go to the Grant Hotel. Thank you." I climb in the cab as the cabbie gets my luggage from the rental car trunk. Once we start towards downtown I rest my head on the back of the seat and close my eyes. Next thing I know the cabbie is banging on the window. I must have fallen asleep. I am a little tired from the trip. I just smile and hand the gentleman his fare and a tip. "Thank you Ned."

4

"Maysen your pager's going off again!"

"Carter why don't you get off your butt and go take the tow? I did the last three!"

"Dude, I'm the one moving to Tulsa with you remember. Least you could do is let me live the last little bit of Omaha nightlife before we leave." He smiles and continues to get ready for another night out and another different woman.

I just shake my head and put on my Rod's Towing hat and head for the door. Climbing into the tow truck and I realize that I won't miss this at all. Won't miss the late night calls and having to go work my butt off and then go to work in the morning too. I'm dead tired and no one seems to care.

Pulling off the highway and turning around to reach the rental car that I was instructed to pick up, I see no one's in it. They must have called a cab and went to the hotel. Smart people, that's for sure. No one around makes these calls go much faster.

****

I took the rental car to the garage and when I get into the passenger seat to get the information out of the glove box, I see an envelope with a school district logo on it and ITINERARY written in the middle. Whomever this belongs to must need it back and when I open the envelope I find a receipt for a hotel room inside. The Grant Hotel. At least I know where I can call to get the envelope to the owner. I pull out my cell phone and dial the hotel number listed on the receipt.

"Yes, I'm looking for a guest you have tonight that's there from a school district. Oh you're full of teachers and administrators? Oh my. Well, she rented a car and it broke down outside of town. Yes, she left her itinerary inside the car. Yes, it had all kinds of paperwork inside. No, the name I see is Joanna Simms. Do you have anyone by that name? Great. Could you connect me to her room? Thank you so much." I wait for the envelope owner to answer and when she does I'm surprised she sounds so young. I had envisioned a cranky old teacher not a young one.

"Yes, ma'am I'm from Rod's Towing and I'm the one who towed your rental car. I found an envelope inside that had a bunch of paperwork I thought you might need. If you'd like I could bring it by the hotel on my way home."

"Oh no, no need for that. Are you far from the hotel? I could just walk there before dinner. Would that be ok?"

"Sure ma'am. If you would prefer to pick it up that's fine. We're actually right around the corner from the Grant so it shouldn't be too hard for you to find us. Rod's Garage. Ok see you in a few."

"Thank you again sir." And she disconnects the line. Why did I offer to wait for her? It's a Tuesday night and I would like to be home packing instead of waiting around for some cranky teacher to retrieve her paperwork. But while I wait I'll finish up a job from earlier today. Might as well get something done while I wait right?

****

I waited for almost two hours and no one came to get an envelope. I got tired of waiting and went home. I guess it wasn't that important after all. Oh well, not my loss.

Driving into work this morning and I can't help but be a little cranky after last night's events. I waited and no one else cared to show up. I took the tow and no one else cared to show up to help. I really won't miss this place. Or the people. I get to work on the next work order hanging in my bay and before I know it it's almost lunch time. My stomach is growling so I take a break and head for the vending machine. I walk inside the break room and sit down to munch on my chips. Just as I get the bag opened and one chip in my mouth I hear Carter calling my name. I growl a little and head for the garage floor again.

"What the hell do you want man? I was just sitting down to have a bite to eat!" I say very annoyed with my friend.

"Dude, some teacher is here to get an envelope. She said she talked to someone who towed the car last night. Since you were the one to do it I thought you might want to talk to her. She's over there by the counter. And she's HOT dude!" I shake my head knowing he would think anyone with female organs was hot. I turn and walk towards the front of the office. I enter the room and about fall flat on my face when I see her standing there.

Audrey. Oh my heavens how in the world can this be her? Here? In Omaha and at Rod's?

"Audrey? Is that you?" I say as I walk towards her. Carter was right, she was HOT. But I already knew that because she's what I see every night when I close my eyes.

"Maysen? Oh my goodness what are you doing here?"

"I work here. What are you doing here?"

"You towed my rental car and I fell asleep before I could come get the envelope last night. I'm very sorry I didn't make it. I hope you didn't wait long."

"Oh no, I didn't stay but a few minutes. What are you doing in Omaha?"

"I'm here for the teacher's conference at the Grant. We're on a lunch break right now so I thought it would be a good time to come get the envelope. I thought you lived in Tulsa?"

"No, I've lived here in Omaha for about six years now. I can't believe you're here. How long will you be in Omaha?"

"I leave tomorrow. I can't believe I ran into you. How's your mom?"

"She's good. Getting out of the hospital next week actually."

"She's been in there this whole time? Is she well again?"

"Yes, she's been battling pneumonia and her COPD has been making that difficult to do. As soon as they get it about cleared up she gets it again. This time they hope she's on the mend and can go home."

"That's awful. I pray she does stay well this time."

"Thank you. Here's the envelope from the car."

"Oh thank you. I need the paperwork for the conference. They told me I could bring it back once I was able to get it from you. Well, not you but from the garage. I didn't know it was you. Are you the one who called me last night?"

"Yes, but I think we were both too tired to realize who we were talking to."

"I never even dreamed it was you."

"Me neither. Would you like to go to dinner with me tonight? I'm done around six and can come pick you up around seven. That is if you don't have anyone here with you."

"No, I'm here alone. I would love that Maysen. I really would."

"Ok I will see you tonight at seven."

"It's a date. Well, maybe not a date, anyway I'll see you then." She blushes and smiles trying to hide her uneasiness.

I smile and touch her arm, "It's a date Audrey. See you then."

I watch her walk out the door and back around the corner towards her hotel. I am so smitten and unaware of my surroundings that I don't hear Carter and Rod come up behind me.

"That is one gorgeous ass if I have ever seen one! Shoooeeey!" I hear Rod say and it makes my blood run hot.

"How dare you talk about her like that you sleaze. Don't you have any respect for women at all?" And I stomp off afraid to hear the comeback and even more afraid of what I would reply with next.

"Dude, what was that all about? You got kinda protective of someone you don't even know. You know that's how Rod is. Why the attitude?"

"I do know her Carter. That was Audrey!"

"The mystery chick from Tulsa? What the heck is she doing here in Omaha? How did she find you?"

"I towed her rental car last night. She left an envelope in it. I didn't have a clue it was her until I walked in the front room and she was standing there. She didn't know I lived here either."

"Dude, did you get her number this time? This is totally fate telling you something!"

"No Carter I didn't get her number."

"You are a lost cause!"

"But I did ask her to dinner. I pick her up at 7." I smile and have a little pep in my step now knowing I'll see her again in a couple of hours.

"That is awesome man!! Do I get to go too so I can check her out?"

"Hell no Carter! She's only here until tomorrow and I don't want to share her you idiot!"

"You go man! Get the girl! Maybe then you'll quit pouting all the time." He slaps me on the back and walks back to his bay and gets back to work. Which is something I should do too so that I can get out of here sooner rather than later. I can't wait to see Audrey again. This is unbelievable that she's here in Omaha. She looks more beautiful than I remember from the hospital. I didn't think that was possible.

5

"Leah, Karlie I have never been this nervous about a dinner before in my life! I can't believe he's here in Omaha! No wonder you never found him online because you looked in the wrong city, heck the wrong state!"

"Just calm down Aud, Karlie and I are here. Well, not there but here and we'll talk you through this. It's just dinner right? If it goes well do you think you'll bring him back to your room? Do you think you'll extend your trip?"

"Leah I have no idea what to expect. We are going to dinner that is all I know. I can't extend my trip. I have a classroom full of second graders that I haven't seen much since last week. I have lesson plans and tests to grade. I'm so far behind it's ridiculous."

"You're making excuses Audrey. Leah and I think you should extend. It will be one more day of school. Then you could have three more days with "Grease Boy" to know if it's what you thought it was back in Tulsa."

"His name is Maysen by the way. And I really can't jump

25

that far ahead without even knowing if we'll hit it off like we did then. It could have been the emotions from the baby and his mom."

"If you say so. You did get the dress I sent to your room didn't you?"

"Yes Karlie I did. You two are terrible. It's red and short and tight!"

"That's perfect. You'll knock his socks off and he won't know what hit him. He may kidnap you and never let you leave his bed!"

"Leah! You're supposed to be the sensible one here. You're turning more into Karlie every day!"

"Just enjoy the evening Aud. You may or may not see this man again. But word to the wise, if you like him, GET HIS NUMBER!" I hear them chime in at the same time.

"Yes mothers. I will talk to you tonight. And if not tonight then tomorrow in the morning." I smile knowing they just screamed when I hung up because they have no idea what's going to happen tonight either. Could I really bring him to my room and sleep with him? I've never done anything even close to that before. I'm not sure I would have the gumption to even offer.

I look at myself in the mirror and can't believe who I see. This is a hot woman that looks ready to knock someone dead with one look. Goodness this sure isn't who I'm used to seeing. I would prefer sweats and a tank top to this halter dress that's so tight I'm not sure I can sit down in it.

Karlie and Leah thought of everything. There are even stilettos in silver and a silver clutch. How in the world did they get all of this found and delivered in a few hours? They're superwomen I guess.

I look one more time in the mirror and figure it's the best I can do. I just pray he likes it and doesn't think I look like a hooker. Oh goodness he won't think I'm a hooker will he? Karlie and Leah I'm going to wring your necks when I get home. He better like this or your husbands are going to be widowers at young ages! I smile knowing my brothers would have heart attacks if they saw me right now. They would kill their wives too if they knew they had arranged the outfit. Smiling and trying to swallow the doubt and fear, I open my room door and head for the elevator. Floor 4, 3, 2, 1, Open. Deep breath.

****

"I have never been this nervous about a date in my life man."

"It will be fine. She agreed to dinner so she obviously wants to see you again, just relax dude."

"You sure use that word a lot anymore. I hope it stays here in Omaha when we move."

"Haha. I think it makes me look cool. Hip. You know, the girls all like the hipsters."

"You're terrible. You keep telling yourself that. I'm going to go meet a real woman with real taste. You have fun with your floozies."

"Think you'll be home tonight?"

"Don't wait up on my account but I haven't a clue what to expect. I don't sleep around you know that. Who knows what tonight's going to bring. See you when I see you." I wink and walk out the front door full of fear and emotions I can't explain.

Once I get to the Grant Hotel I stand in front of the elevator. It's a little before seven and my stomach is doing flips. I see the numbers light up and count down from five. And it opens.

Holy shit. That is the most gorgeous woman I have ever laid my eyes on. Red dress and silver heels. Oh my goodness am I alive? As soon as she sees me she smiles and I know it's real. I know this beauty before me is real. And here to meet me. Plain old me. I won't complain.

"Audrey you look amazing. Absolutely beautiful."

"You don't think it's too much? My sisters in law arranged for the dress and shoes to be delivered when I told them I had a dinner date."

"Remind me to thank them if I ever have the pleasure of meeting them. You took my breath away."

"Thank you Maysen you're so kind."

"Kind? No, I'm in awe. And a red blooded American male." I whistle and twirl her around so I can get a better look at her. I feel as if I should be wiping drool off my face. This woman is spectacular.

"Well thank you. I'm not used to dressing like this so I'm a little uncomfortable. I feel like it's too much."

"No way. Are you ready to eat though? I'm ready to get you alone and away from all the male stares."

"Oh Maysen you're silly. No one is looking at me and I hope this dress allows me to sit down." She laughs hesitantly and takes my arm as we walk towards the restaurant. I can't help but look around at all the eyes staring at my date. My chest swells up with pride knowing she's with me tonight. And I have intention of letting anyone else take her.

****

"So, how long have you lived in Omaha?"

"I moved here to go to college and have been here since. So, almost 8 years I think? Makes me sound old putting it that way."

"You're not old. You definitely don't look it."

"Well thank you. How long have you been a teacher?"

"Almost 6 years. I went to college in Tulsa and went straight to teaching from there. I really love it. Seeing those little faces light up when they start to get it."

"You really do love it. Your whole face lit up when you were talking about your job. That's great that you found your calling."

"You don't like being a mechanic? That is what you went to school for right?"

"Yes, that's what I went to school for but I also have my Bachelor's in business too so one day I hope to own my own shop."

"Here in Omaha?"

"I really don't know. The right opportunity hasn't presented itself yet. I don't like the moron I work for now, but it's a job ya know?"

"I do know. I am very blessed to have gotten the position I have now. The current second grade teacher decided not to come back from maternity leave so they asked me to stay on full time. Well, that was 5 years ago. I'm sure one day you'll find your opportunity, as you put it."

"Anyway, enough about work. When do you leave?"

"Tomorrow, late morning. I have a taxi coming to get me since my rental is broken. They wanted to give me another; I just refused and said I would get a cab. I don't like driving in the big city. Scares me."

"Small town girl huh?"

"Yes. That obvious huh?"

"You seem so sweet and innocent that you couldn't have been corrupted by the big city. And of course you're not liking to drive in traffic. Dead giveaway."

"You have a good sense about me because I have always been the "good girl" and never been wild or reckless. I wouldn't know what reckless was if it hit me over the head." I smile and think how I would love to get wild and reckless with him. Audrey, my goodness what has gotten into you? Tight dress and champagne aren't a good combination for you. I smile anyway knowing whatever happens in this town will stay here. It was a chance encounter twice; a third time would be ludicrous.

"Never been wild? Even in high school or college?"

"I have three older brothers so they never allowed me to be wild and crazy growing up. Then in college I was never able to get crazy either because I was studying so much. Maybe a little too much. Kind of an overachiever." I shrug my shoulders knowing I'm exactly that.

"Three older brothers. I bet they were wild and crazy. Well, what would you like to do that's so wild and reckless Miss Audrey?"

"Goodness I don't have a clue. What do you wild and reckless people do to have a good time?"

Chuckling I hear him say, "I am the wrong one to ask. I work so much myself I don't get wild and crazy. Whenever I have time it's usually spent checking in on my Mom. It was just she and I growing up. She worked all the time and so did I to help out where I could."

"Classic single mother story I take it? Works herself to the bone to provide for her children and the children in turn take care of her once they are grown?"

"Guilty. My Mom has been sick for so long now that I've really been thinking of moving her up here now. She isn't as happy.

Still tries to be independent."

"She has always been independent and that would be taking it away from her. I can understand that."

"Me too. It's just hard having her so far away. Goodness how did we get onto another boring story? Back to your wild and reckless life." He winks and lifts his glass to his lips. I see his throat move as he swallows. Good grief Audrey, not like you have never seen a man drink before. Get a grip on yourself!

"Would you like dessert ma'am?" I hear the waitress come and ask from beside me. Thankfully something to distract me from this beautiful man in front of me.

"I don't know. What do you think Maysen?"

"How about two pieces of chocolate to go?" he says and wiggles his eye brows at me. What in the world does that mean? I feel the nerves start to bubble up in my stomach. This is all my fault. I was flirting and now he thinks I am that kind of girl.

"I don't know about that I have to get up early tomorrow."

"It's only cake. You can take yours and I'll take mine. No worries. No strings. Just cake." He says smiling with a sparkle still in his eye. I can tell he's trying not to smile.

"Ok that will work thank you. Dinner has gone so quickly. I think I inhaled it or someone else was stealing it off my plate." I smile knowing that sounds so lame.

"Time flies when you're having fun. At least that is what Mom's has always told me. I have had a lot of fun talking to you tonight. Thank you for having dinner with me." Maysen reaches across the table and takes my hand in his. His hand feels like it's electrified as he rubs my mine with his thumb. I feel as if my hair should be standing on end from being electrocuted.

"I have had a wonderful time too. Just wish I weren't

leaving tomorrow."

"Do you have to leave tomorrow? Or can you stay longer?"

"I have to get back. I have barely been home in the past week or so and have a ton of grading to do."

"Sounds exciting."

"I really don't mind it. Overachiever, remember?"

"Funny. I like that about you though. You know what you want and you work very hard to get it."

"Too hard sometimes and the world goes on without me."

"Would you like to go for a walk before turning in?"

"I would love to. Let me freshen up first and we can go." I stand up to head to the bathroom but I guess the champagne has gotten to me more than I thought. I stumble a bit with these high heels on but Maysen easily stands up and slips his arms around my waist to steady me. I look up into his dark eyes and feel as if I'm falling into a bottomless pit. No end in sight.

"Are you ok? You're going to kill yourself in those heels Audrey." He sounds strained as he says that. His eyes are darkening even more with the desire he has while holding me so close. Neither of us pulls away instead we continue to stare at each other not saying a word.

After a few breaths I realize just what I must look like standing here in this getup with a man holding me in front of the whole restaurant. "I'm so sorry about that. I must have had too much champagne."

"You had one glass Audrey, nothing to apologize for. I'm sorry I shouldn't have held onto you like that. I thought you were going to fall so I just reacted. Again, I'm sorry." He lets go and backs up leaving me still standing here like an idiot lusting after him.

"No, without you I would have fallen and probably broken my ankle or my neck. Thank you. I'm going to try to make it to the restroom now. Excuse me." And I practically run to the bathroom. I'm so humiliated I can't stand it.

As soon as I get the door shut I dial Karlie's number. "Audrey, what's wrong? What's happening?"

"Karlie, I should kill you two. I have about killed myself in these contraptions you call shoes several times already tonight!"

"What did Prince Charming think of the dress? Besides, you gave me a dress close to that for my bachelorette party!"

"I think he appreciated it. His eyes about bugged out of his head."

"Mission accomplished then! That was the point Audrey!"

"Yes but now what do I do? He wants to go for a walk but I'm scared. I don't know what to do in this situation."

"You do know how to walk right? Last I knew a walk meant a walk goofball."

"Yes, but after that silly. What do I do after we get back? What if he asks to come to my room or something? What do I do then?"

"Good grief Audrey, I'm not going to map the night out for you. What you do with the night is up to you. Be brave and do something you would never do. You might be surprised with yourself and enjoy every minute of it."

"I could be over reacting too right? Maybe he really is just wanting to take a walk right?"

"Yes Audrey, it could be just that. But by the way you said he liked the dress I'm sure walking is not all that's on his mind. Just roll with it. Go with the flow and take your queues from him."

"That's what I'm afraid of Karlie. I have never just been with a man without being in a relationship for a while first. I don't want Maysen to think I'm easy or anything."

"He won't Audrey. If he has learned anything about you it's that you're a wholesome small town good girl. He likes that about you I'm sure."

"Just go with the flow huh? I'll try to do that but Karlie, stay by the phone. I might have to call you."

"Don't keep Prince Charming waiting any longer. Go. Do something daring. Live your life Audrey. We love you."

"Ok. Bye."

"Call me as soon as you get in tonight. I'll be waiting."

"I'm sure you will." I laugh and hang up the phone trying to calm the tidal wave of fear that's welling up inside my stomach. I take a deep breath and hold it for a few seconds. Letting it out I open the bathroom door and pat down my dress to ensure it's covering the key body parts still.

On shaky legs I walk to the front of the restaurant where I see Prince Charming, as Karlie called him, waiting for me. His eyes are glued on me as if I were a special prize he couldn't wait to win. Tidal wave number two comes rolling in. Oh boy.

6

"What's wrong? Am I trailing toilet paper from my shoe or what?" I say turning to make sure I don't actually have the toilet paper coming from my shoe. That would be embarrassing. Like standing here in this getup isn't embarrassing? Audrey shut up.

"N-n-nothing is wrong actually. You are gorgeous. I can't believe you're leaving with me. Hell even talking to me." I can see a slight reddening come across his handsome face. How sweet.

"Oh stop it. I'm not comfortable talking about this. Are you ready for that walk now?" He extends his elbow and I place my hand just inside the fold. He pulls me closer to his side and I visualize sparks shooting between our bodies. I roll my eyes and shake it off. I'm getting delusional now. Snap out of it Audrey, good grief.

"Have you seen the pond and trails at the park across the street from the hotel?"

"No, but I would love to."

Maysen directs us in the direction of the park entrance and I see there are many couples inside that seem to have the same idea we do. Some might have a little bit more on their minds at the moment than we do. Scratch that maybe it's the same. They look a lot more comfortable with the idea than we do. Oh brother Audrey, you would think you've never been with a man before. You're acting like a teenager with your first crush.

"Can I hold your hand? If that's not too much to ask." I nod and allow his big fingers to slide between mine, every last hot one. The moment his touch mine, I feel my temperature spike again. What is this, tidal wave twenty?

We walk on the path for a few minutes both silent and afraid to speak. I don't want to say anything stupid enough to make him change his mind about spending time with me tonight. I'm good at that. Aiden and Aaron always made fun of me as a kid because I could trip over my own words more often than not.

"You're quiet. Are you ok?" He squeezes my hand and I feel another spark shoot through me. This man's simple actions are driving me insane. I don't know how to deal with this new situation.

"I'm just fine. You fine?" Dummy that sounds intelligent. "I mean, are you ok? You're quiet too."

He smiles a gentle and warm smile but stops in front of me and takes both hands in his. I look up into those amazing eyes and can't help but look at his perfectly formed lips. Out of instinct I think I licked my own lips as I did so because his eyes slipped down to them. His smile fades just as he realizes we are both thinking of the same thing. A kiss. He leans down and hesitates just before his lips touch mine. I close my eyes and lean the rest of the way to meet him.

Electricity! Heaven! I think I'm going to faint. Holy crap!

****

Audrey's lips on mine, the most perfect feeling in the entire world. I have never felt so much emotion and electricity kissing any other woman. Duh, it's never been this beautiful, intelligent and HOT woman in front of me.

I can feel her sway as if she's losing her footing so of course I did what every man would do; I wrap my arms around her waist to give her my support. Any man would do that right? Who cares you fool, you like this girl, go for it! If she pulls away, she pulls away and you'll know where you stand. You have to try or you'll never know again.

Hallelujah she didn't pull away; instead her hands are on my chest now. They're making their way to my neck. That simple action makes me feel as if I'm floating on air and the world has slipped away except for me and Audrey. Oh good grief you idiot you sound like a girl. But it's true this feels like Heaven.

After Audrey's hand snake behind my head and fill with my hair and pull me closer to her, I lose my self-control. Completely lose myself.

Running my tongue along her lips I feel them part and her own tongue come out to meet mine. Tasting her sweet mouth and the wine from dinner mixed in there sends my pulse in over-drive. More than it already was I guess. I didn't realize it could beat any faster, but it just might beat out of my chest.

She shivers and lets out a slight moan that my tongue takes as a go-ahead and delves into her waiting mouth. Her tongue meets mine taste for taste. I tilt her head to give gain better access and hear myself let out a matching sound. I could stand here in this park with this woman for the rest of my life.

Park. Park. You're in a public park pawing at this poor woman you moron! I retract my rogue tongue and tighten my grip on her to allow my brain to start working again. It's as if I'm swimming in emotions I never knew were possible.

"What's wrong? Did I do something wrong? I'm sorry I

shouldn't have done that." She pulls away and rights her shirt starting to redden with embarrassment. She's fumbling to keep her attention away from me.

"Audrey, I'm so sorry I just did that to you in public. That was far beyond uncalled for. I let myself get carried away and should never have done that. Please don't think there was anything you did wrong. I am completely to blame." I reach up and rub my hand along her cheek. My heart lets out its own sigh as I do so. This woman is just so amazing and she sets my body on fire.

"Don't apologize, I was there too. I'm as much to blame. I did love every minute of it." She reddens and looks at the ground again.

I lift her chin up so that her eyes look straight at me and I say, "That was the most memorable kiss I have ever had. With anyone. Ever. I wouldn't mind doing it again. But preferably away from public eyes." I smile hoping to ease her embarrassment and let her know I'm serious.

"Would you like to come back to my room for a drink?" I think I must be hearing things now. There is no way she just asked me back to her room. No way.

****

I ask him back to my room and he has a look of shock on his face and not saying anything. Great, that kissing and attacking I did just now ruined everything.

"I'm sorry that was too forward. I'm going to go now, thank you so much for dinner and your company. It was great to catch up with you again. Take care Maysen." And I turn to walk away. I can't believe this is happening. I'm the world's biggest moron. Amazing man and I ruin it by being too eager and crazed. Karlie and Leah are too deep in my head.

As I'm turning to walk away in shame, I feel his hand wrap

around my arm and pull me back his way. I look at him in confusion. He's scowling, that can't be a good sign.

"I would like NOTHING more than to go back to your room for a drink Audrey. Never doubt how I feel about you." And he walks quickly back towards my hotel dragging me behind. Okay maybe not dragging me but he is in a fast walk which makes me feel dragged behind because his long legs take much bigger strides than mine.

I'm out of breath before we reach the entrance to the hotel. I stop and lean against the wall right inside the front doors and pull my hand out of his. He realizes what I'm doing and does the only thing that could have surprised me tonight. He picks me up in his arms and runs up the stairs to my room.

"Which room?"

"212. You don't have to carry me, I can walk. I just needed a breather." I try to wiggle out of his hold but he tightens the hold diminishing any chance of my escape.

"Key? Where is it?"

"Right here in my purse." I start to fumble with my purse and feel my pulse quicken as I touch the slick plastic key card. I take it out and as I do he leans forward to allow me access to the door. Swiping the card with shaking hands, I get it done and the light turns green. Before I know it, the door is ripped open and we're inside. Maysen lets go of my legs and swings me so that my body is horizontal against his but my legs are wrapped around his midsection. He presses me against the now closed door and kisses my lips so fast and hard that I feel as if the breath has been sucked out of me. But once his heat reaches through my clothes, other feelings and an entirely different reaction comes flooding in.

"Are you sure about this Audrey? I won't be able to stop if we go any further. If you're not, please tell me now. I won't make you do anything you don't want to do." He looks straight into my eyes.

I knew in that moment that I didn't need to think about this. For the first time in my life I know exactly what I want and I'm not holding back. I pull him closer and kiss him like there's no tomorrow. That should get my answer across.

7

I awake with the sun streaming in a crack in the curtains. I must not have gotten them shut last night before dinner. I'm sure regretting that now. It's going right across my eyes and nowhere else of course. I was in too big of a hurry to get downstairs to meet Maysen. A slow smile goes across my lips as I remember how handsome he looked in his suit. And the look on his face when he saw me it made me feel so beautiful. And last night after our walk...

OH MY GOSH MAYSEN! I slowly move my head to the left and see his handsome face and oh so hot body lying next to mine. His arm lying across my stomach. In my bed. Oh my gosh. Oh my gosh. He's still here. In my bed. Oh my gosh.

I turn my head back away from him and panic. Full on panic. I have to look dreadful! Dreadful morning breath!! Oh my gosh. He will run for the hills if he sees what I look like in the morning! I cup my hand around my mouth and blow trying to smell my breath and oh my goodness. That's atrocious! My hair has to be a mess and my makeup! I didn't wash my face last night. I jump out of bed and reach for my robe. Throwing it on I rush to the bathroom in dire need of some fixing.

As I reach the bathroom and shut the door I get the first

glimpse of my horrendous appearance. Holy crap! I look as if I had quite the wild night and got hit by a bus while at it! I can't let Maysen see me like this! He'll chew his own arm off to get away from me. I splash water on my face, lather up the soap and scrub like there's no tomorrow. A clean face looks 100% better than the one I had before. I comb my hair until it's manageable and doesn't look too terrible. Teeth. Gotta brush my teeth. Crap! My toothbrush is in my bag. But my bag is out there on the chair. On the chair by the bed. The bed with Maysen in it. Oh my goodness hot Maysen that's naked. Well I imagine he's naked. I was when I woke up so he has to be right? Men don't get up and get dressed if they stay all night do they? Oh my goodness I am so naïve I have no idea. But I need my toothbrush. I'll just hurry, get it and be back to brush my teeth. Then I'll crawl back into that bed with him and see where the day goes! Sounds easy right?

I open the bathroom door a crack and sneak a quick peek to make sure Maysen is still asleep. But as I do I hear a door shut. The door to the room. I look at the bed again and see that there's nothing there but the mangled sheets from a wild night between two people that threw caution to the wind. And no Maysen.

He left. My world starts to swirl around me as I realize that he must have been so ashamed of what we did that he snuck out the second he was free to do so. He didn't even say goodbye. Oh gosh was I that terrible?

How could I have done this? This is why I never veer off the straight and narrow. It's just not for me. What have I done? I thought we had such a strong connection! Why did I listen to Karlie and Leah? Why did I let them doubt who I am or who I'm supposed to be? Great. Just great.

****

As I wake I can feel Audrey's silky warm skin underneath my arm. I open my eyes and see her beautiful face right there next to me. I could get used to seeing that face and feeling her lying by my side. After last night there's nowhere else I would rather be than here with this woman. It's never felt so right being with someone or touching someone like that before.

I can feel Audrey stir and I close my eyes so that she doesn't catch me staring at her. I feel her lift my arm off of her and she gets out of bed. I open my eyes and see her sit up searching for clothing. What I wouldn't give to hook my arm around her waist and bring her back against me to have a recap of what we did last night. Her body is so perfect and her creamy skin just makes my mouth water.

She gets a robe on and makes a bee line for the bathroom. She practically ran as fast as she could. Ran away from me. That makes my heart hurt. She ran away from me and what we did. She is ashamed of us and what happened between us. My heart just dropped into my stomach. I never thought she didn't want that. I thought we were on the same page and had that connection that everyone talks about. I guess I was wrong. She couldn't get away from me fast enough!

I can't be laying here when she comes back out of the bathroom. I can't see the look of shame and disappointment on her face. I should have known a good girl like her couldn't do what we did and be ok with herself in the morning. But I don't want to leave her. I might never see her again and that breaks my heart.

I climb out of the disaster that are the sheets and covers and dress as quickly as I can. The whole time my heart is heavy and I'm confused as to what I should do. Do I wait and see if she's ok or just leave and save her the act of rejecting me? I can't handle the rejection. I'll just leave before she comes out and no harm with be done. Right? So why is this killing me?

I put on my last boot and head for the door. I pause at the bathroom door wanting to say goodbye to Audrey but I hear water running. She must be washing away the memories from what we did together. I open the room door and walk out. Walk out leaving the most beautiful and wonderful woman I have ever met behind.

Behind and may never see again.

****

"Karlie, you two were wrong. I did what you said and now he's left disgusted with me."

"What do you mean disgusted? Did he tell you that?"

"No, I went to the bathroom before he woke up to brush my teeth and wash my face and when I came back out he was gone. Without a word."

"Audrey, I'm so sorry! I never thought he would be one to do that to you. I just knew you two had that special connection. I'm so sorry honey."

"I thought we did too, that's why I threw caution to the wind and slept with him. Look where that got me!"

"Audrey, you need to take a hot shower, pack and head home. Your flight leaves this morning right?"

"Yes, it leaves at eleven. I'm going to shower and I'll let you know when I'm home. I just can't believe this is happening. I was honestly thinking of extending my trip a few days so I could stay with Maysen a little longer. Clearly I was delusional about what we had. He wanted me for a bed partner but nothing else. Good grief Karlie I must have been horrible last night. What have I done?"

"Audrey, everyone makes mistakes. You followed your heart instead of your head. There is nothing to be ashamed of. You have been walking the straight and narrow with no look outside the box until now. This is just a set back today. Tomorrow you'll be just fine and everything will be better once you get home. Put Omaha behind you."

"And Tulsa. What are the odds that I run into him here too? Twice Karlie. Twice. How was this not our second chance? Karlie I just can't believe things went so badly this morning."

"Honey, I wish I were there to hug you right now. Just take a deep breath and take a long hot shower. You'll feel better. I promise. Get on that plane and come home. We'll be waiting for you."

"Thanks Karlie. And please don't say anything to my brothers about this? That would be terrible. They would want to hunt him down and commit murder. Even though he hurt me he doesn't deserve the wrath of the Blake brothers. See you when I get home."

I hang up the phone and take that suggested deep breath. I fight back the tears and head for the shower. A long hot one should help ease my tense muscles for sure. But can it wash away this pain?

****

I've been sitting here across the street from the hotel since I walked out this morning. I just can't leave here knowing Audrey is in there feeling like she does. I had intended on inviting her to spend the morning with me until it was time for her to fly home. I've seen couples go in and out of those front doors but no Audrey. And definitely not me with her as one of those happy couples. She said her flight leaves at eleven so she should be about ready to hail a cab and head out of my life for good. That just makes me sick to think about. Never seeing her again? Why did this happen this way? What went wrong? I'll never know.

"Hey Carter, I need your advice. I messed up and I'm not sure what I did or what to do."

"What's up man? How was the big date? I see you didn't come home last night so it must have gone well?"

"It was amazing. The night was too. But this morning is when it all fell apart."

"What happened dude? Did she laugh at your ugly mug this morning?"

"I really don't know what happened. I was looking at her while she was sleeping and then she stirred and practically ran to the bathroom. When I realized she was ashamed of what we did, I got dressed and left before she could come out."

"Dude, you just left? Didn't even say goodbye? You are a moron."

"I didn't want her to have to deal with seeing me if she was so ashamed and stuff. Carter, you're supposed to be helping me feel better, not worse."

"Look man, I know you really like this girl, but maybe it's best. You said she wasn't from here so it's not like you're going to see her again. Right? Or did you exchange info this time?"

"Crap! No, I didn't get her number. Again. I can't believe I didn't get it this time either."

"You were a little preoccupied, if you know what I mean."

"I can see that annoying eye brow thing you're doing from here. Don't talk about her like that. Or I'll kick your butt to next week."

"Whoa dude, you're grumpy this morning. Just come home and get some rest. Obviously you didn't get much last night and now you're ready to kill anyone who looks at you wrong."

"Funny. I actually slept better with her in my arms than I think I ever have. Until she ran away horrified. This sucks dude!!"

"Go back in there and talk to the girl or like I said, come home."

"Why did I call you again?" I hang up the phone, throw it across the car and look towards the hotel entrance again.

And as I do the person who has been occupying the majority of my thoughts since yesterday comes walking out looking gorgeous.

I watch her get into a cab and then escape out of my life. For good this time. Wish my heart didn't break at that thought.

8

Six months later

"Audrey, open up!" I hear them yelling from the front door. I knew locking it when I got in last night was a good idea. If I ignore them long enough they'll go away. I hope. It's been about four and a half months since I got back from Omaha and the hurt's only beginning to ease up. I dream about Maysen almost every night but he's never here with me when I wake up breaking my heart all over again.

"Audrey Lucille Blake, open this damned door before I break it down!" Oh my gosh they sent my brothers. What were they thinking? I climb out of bed and groan just to feel that yucky feeling again. I must have the flu. It's only getting worse. I'm going to have to go to the doctor soon and I know my brothers and their wives are going to make the appointment for me if I don't.

"Alright alright. You can stop shouting before dad comes out with the gun."

"Dad knows we're here. They haven't seen much of you either so we're all worried about you." I hear Aiden say as I open the door with a very scary look on my face. But instantly laugh when I see the even scarier looks on my brothers' faces. Little

Audrey's brothers are coming to the rescue again. Like always.

"What do you guys want? I was sleeping. Quite soundly if you need to know." I put my hands on my hips and look at each of them before they answer.

"It's three o'clock in the afternoon Audrey. Why in the world are you still sleeping? Are you sick or what? Ever since we all got home from New York you've been a hermit crab."

"So what? I'm an adult and if I want to sleep all day I can. Last I knew you weren't my boss or my parent. Now, go away."

"You look terrible Audrey. You have bags the size of Texas under your eyes and you're looking almost green. Are you sick?"

"Yes, I've been a little sick the past couple of days if you must know. Now if you'll excuse me, I would like to go back to my bed."

"We're making you an appointment for the doctor and you're going. No excuses." Austin says and pushes through my door and straight to the kitchen.

"When's the last time you've eaten young lady?"

"Austin, I can take care of myself. You have a fiancé to take care of and Aiden you have a wife and baby to take care of. Go do that and leave me alone. I don't need my big brothers to take care of me anymore. Go away!"

"We are not leaving you to mope or whatever you're doing any longer."

"They didn't. They told you? They weren't supposed to do that! Dammit those two are dead when I see them again!"

"Calm down, they didn't give us details. Just that things didn't go your way in Omaha and you came back unhappy. What did happen Audrey? Do we need to go kick someone's ass?"

"Shut up Aiden. I told you two to leave me alone. I don't need nor want you here right now. I'm going to go throw up and then go back to bed. Leave me alone and tell the others to do the same. I'll come out of hiding when I'm ready. Got it?"

"Geez Audrey, we just love you. I'll make you an appointment for tomorrow afternoon. You are going to work aren't you? It's Monday"

"I know what day tomorrow is you idiot. I haven't missed a day of work since I started. Just go away! I can make my own appointment. I'm not a child! Get out!" I scream and once they've stepped out the door I slam it and turn the lock once again.

Aaaaahhhhhhh! Why can't everyone just leave me alone?

I really feel like I could throw up again so I walk to the bathroom. Once I see myself in the mirror I can clearly see why they're concerned. I look like death. Probably worse. Oh well, I feel like that so why wouldn't I look the part?

****

"Maysen, are you going to go see your Mom today? This bar is such a dive. It smells and I always smell like a bar itself when I get home. Today I work the late shift. Sure you don't want me to get you a job too?" He says as he picks up his clothes and throws them into the washing machine. We have a small two bedroom apartment in Tulsa as close to the hospital as we could find. It's tiny to say the least but we can easily afford it and we're guys, we don't care what it looks like.

"Yeah, I'm gonna go see her right now. I doubt I'll like this new job any better than the last one we had but it's not Omaha. And Mom's here so it's worth the move. Right? Hey Carter?"

"What? You gonna confess your undying love for me now or what?"

"Oh shut it you moron. I was only going to say thanks for moving to Tulsa with me. I'm sorry you have to work at that dive bar. You'll find something better soon."

"Dude, I hated Omaha as much as you. I'll find something else, but for right now I don't mind doing something different. And the ladies I see every night. Whoa. That's the perk of the job!"

"You're such a pig. Glad to see you haven't changed." Shaking my head I walk out the door towards my car. Tomorrow I'll be on my way to the new job at the car dealership around the corner from the hospital. It's not my own garage, but it's not Red's either. It's going to be bearable and keep me by Mom.

Things have been strange being back in Tulsa where I met Audrey. I look for her everywhere but I never see her. Every blond woman looks like her until I get closer and it's never her face I see. Only women giving me the stink eye for walking up to them and stopping when I see they aren't who I thought they were. No girl likes to be told they aren't who you're looking for. That I have found out. Been slapped a few times too. Carter finds that the silver lining. Of course he would, he's the one that has women falling at his feet while I don't want anyone but Audrey and know I can't have her.

"Mom, how ya feeling today? Good. I'm headed your way right now. Yes, I do start the new job tomorrow. Yes, I'll stop by after and tell you all about it. Yes I promise. See you in a few. Love you." I hang up and shake my head at how maternal she has been lately. You would think I was a child again. She calls me five times a day and always wants to hear about every move I make. She even guessed there was a girl that broke my heart. If only I could have introduced her to Audrey. I breathe in deep and slowly let it out. Hoping memories and pictures of Audrey will leave too. No such luck.

****

"Miss Blake? Are you feeling ok? You look pale." I hear a

voice from my classroom doorway. Leaning up against it is Miss Woods, the fifth grade teacher from down the hall.

I smile and nod my head. "I have a doctor appointment in a few minutes. I'm not sure what's wrong with me but I just don't feel right."

"Do you need someone to drive you? You really don't look well."

"I'll be fine. Thank you." I stand up to leave and about pass out. What the heck is wrong with me? Wonder if I have an ear infection? My equilibrium is definitely off. And those leftovers must have been bad that I ate too.

I walk to my car and head towards the doctor's office. As I pull up there I see Aiden's pickup parked there by the front doors. Oh you have got to be kidding me! And now he's walking towards me with Austin in tow. What in the world is this?

"What are you two doing here? I can go to the doctor all by myself! I am not a child and I DO NOT NEED YOU TWO!" I storm off but when I reach the front door to the building I turn around and glare at my brothers who are still standing there looking dumbfounded. They throw their hands up and get in the pickup. I stand there glaring until they drive away. Good grief I can't even go to the doctor by myself? What am I twelve? Once I see they're gone I continue in and fill out more paperwork that I've ever seen in one sitting.

"Audrey Blake."

I hear my name called and look up to see the nurse is ready to take me back to see the doctor. Let's find out just what is making me so sick. Food poisoning would not surprise me since I haven't wanted to eat anything but leftovers Mom has been bringing me lately. I just don't like being around the whole family, especially the happy couples that seem to be everywhere you turn in the house.

Living in the apartment above the garage at the 6AB has given me the freedom I need but also letting me have the close proximity to my family. Well that is until they come pounding on my door and waking me up! Nosy family members make me want to move to town and on my own. Maybe that's what I need to do. Ugh I just don't want to do that. I would really be alone then.

"I'm Audrey." She directs me down a hallway with doors on both sides of me.

"Fourth door on your right please. I'll take your height and weight when we get in there. Along with your blood pressure."

"Thank you." When we get inside and she shuts the door I step onto the scale hoping I'm able to sit down soon because I'm feel yucky again.

"Ok Audrey, sit down and we'll get started. Can you tell me what's been going on with you? And how long?"

"Sure. I have been starting to feel nasty a couple of days ago. It comes and goes really. I think it was just something I ate and an ear infection because my equilibrium is off."

"Have you been throwing up and getting dizzy every day? All day?"

"No, it seems to come and go. I am usually feeling the worst in the morning but the dizziness seems to come whenever I stand up too quickly."

"Have you been having stomach pains along with the vomiting?"

"No. Just can't seem to keep anything down."

"I see. Well, I think we are going to draw a little blood and run some tests that will help us to determine just what is wrong with you. I'll send the phlebotomist in soon. Please just sit tight and there's a trash can over there if you need it. Hope you get to feeling better Audrey."

"Thank you, me too." Before I know another lady comes and draws my blood and once again I'm sitting in the exam room alone waiting for the doctor.

After about ten minutes of sitting in the room alone I lie back and doze off a bit. Before I could get too many zzz's in the doctor entered the room with a smile.

"Miss Blake? I hear you're feeling pretty rough lately?"

"Yes. Are my tests back?"

"Actually yes they are. I'm going to do a little exam but I do believe I know what's causing your illness. We'll wait until I'm done examining you to go over that."

I just look at him and nod. What else am I going to, throw a fit and demand the answers now? I've been sitting here long enough to let them cut off an arm if needed.

"Now, Miss Blake. We ran some tests on the blood that was taken and the tests came back positive. You're going to be a mother in a few months." He looks at me smiling and expecting me to smile back. When I don't he creases his brows and leans forward. "Are you ok? I take it you weren't expecting a baby?"

"A b-b-baby? Are you sure? This can't be right." I think back to the only night in a very long time that I had sex. Omaha. Maysen. Oh my goodness. This can't be happening. I drop my head into my hands and let the tears flow that have been threatening me for so long. I let it all go and leave nothing left to cry about.

"Miss Blake, do you need me to call someone?"

"No, I'll be fine."

"You'll need to make an appointment with the OBGYN for as soon as you can. It looks like you might be four or five months pregnant and you really need to see one. You probably should have at twelve weeks. Have you not seen any of the signs?"

"No, my period has still been coming and I have felt fine until recently. Are you sure about this? I am on birth control. Isn't that supposed to keep you from getting pregnant? That's the point of it right?"

"Audrey, it's not 100% effective. This is a small miracle that has happened to you. Your boyfriend will be just as surprised and happy won't he?"

"I don't have a boyfriend. The-the-the father doesn't live here."

"Well, on your way out, stop by the OBGYN's window and they'll schedule your appointment. They can give you any information you might need. Good luck and congratulations. Very exciting news! Having children is the biggest accomplishment a person can do."

"Yes, thank you." I jump off the exam table and head back down the hallway full of doors. I feel as if this hallway seems to be getting longer and I'll never reach the end of it. More doors and more doors. Never ending and more doors.

And then I pass out. Completely this time. The nurses and doctors come running and help me carry me to an empty exam room.

"Audrey, can you hear me?"

"Audrey, wake up." Karlie and Leah? What are they doing here? Where is here anyway? I open up my eyes to see an unfamiliar beige ceiling. With a few brown stains on it. Gross where am I? I look around more and see that the walls all match the ceiling color. Then the smell of disinfectant hits my nostrils and I realize that I'm in the hospital.

"Where am I? What are you two doing here?" I sit up and

see my sisters in law standing holding each of my hands.

"You're still in the clinic. You fainted and they brought you in here to lie down. One of the nurses called me and we rushed over here." Karlie says and gives me a big hug.

"I passed out? That's so weird. I don't have the ear infection I thought I did."

"What did they say was wrong with you?"

"Yeah, what did they say? Your brothers said they made you really mad earlier coming by here before your appointment." Leah says and hugs me too.

"I can't believe they showed up here like I couldn't take my own self to the doctor!"

"We told them they were idiots." Karlie says snickering knowing how the scene must have gone down. Little ol' me taking out the big bad Blake brothers.

"How long was I out?"

"They said about twenty minutes. Are you feeling ok now? What did they say was wrong?"

"What's wrong? Everything. I need to go home. Please don't follow me either." I give them hugs and walk out the exam room door this time making it to the end and eventually out the front doors, after briefly stopping to get the OBGYN information. I'll call later, I can't right now. It's not real yet. Once inside my car, I cry again. What am I going to do?

I am pregnant? Pregnant. With Maysen's baby. And I have no clue of how to get ahold of him. This is just freaking wonderful. I see Karlie and Leah standing by their car doors staring at me so I start the engine, wave and drive towards home. My life just drastically took a turn in another direction.

Once home I take a look around and realize that my whole life just changed, every single part of it. I'm going to be a mother in four or five months. Oh my goodness. I am not going to be able to do this alone, but I have no clue how to get in touch with Maysen. But I do need to tell my family. First I'll start with my sisters in law. They can help me tell the others. Aaahhh this is not going to be easy. Miss Perfect Audrey isn't quite so perfect anymore. She got knocked up by a stranger and now raising a child alone. Wow.

****

"Well, I think I'll go get some dinner and go home. I've got to start at the dealership tomorrow."

"Ok honey. I wish you didn't have to work somewhere you don't love. Have you ever thought of opening up your own shop?"

"Of course I've thought about it. It's Carter and I's dream, we just haven't found the right opportunity."

"I really don't like him working at that yucky bar either Son. Can't you get him a job at the dealership?"

"Mom, I barely got the job. I haven't even started yet. He doesn't want to work at the dealership anyway."

"Well, maybe you should move to Colvin and work with Uncle Sam. Aunt Ingrid said he's been wanting to get out of the business and finally retire. It's just a small town and there's no one else to take it over for him. Maybe that's your opportunity you've been talking about Maysen."

"I didn't know he owned the garage, I just thought he worked there. If he's serious about selling it, I might be interested. I'd probably need to go down there and check it out for sure and of course talk to Carter about it."

"It's so good to see your face light up like that again Son. I'll call her as soon as you leave and let you know what she says."

"That would be perfect. Love you Mom. See you tomorrow."

Walking to my car I realize that this might actually be that golden opportunity we've been waiting for. I look at my watch and see that Carter's shift has started so I head to the bar. I'll have a drink and talk to him about this idea.

As I walk into the bar I can see he's already surrounded by floozies. They aren't even clean ones. Good grief man, have some standards.

"Hey man, what's up? I didn't know you were coming in tonight? How's your Mom?"

"She's good. We had a conversation that I wanted to talk to you about."

"Oh yeah, what's that? Let me get these lovely ladies some drinks and I'll be right back with you."

"Pig." That's all I need to say and he smiles and winks like a randy teenager. I roll my eyes and shake my head.

"Ok man, what's up?"

"My Uncle Sam owns a garage in their hometown of Colvin it's about two hours away from here. He's pretty old and wants to retire but no one in town wants to take it over. That's where we might come in. Would you want to come with me to check it out? We could leave Friday after I get off and be back Saturday night before your shift here starts. Unless you wanted to stay all weekend. Mom wants to go too so she can visit with Aunt Ingrid while we talk business."

"Dude, that sounds amazing. I am so in. I'll tell them I won't be back until Sunday. Tanya can take my shift Friday and Saturday. We leave as soon as you're off. This could be it man. I'm excited."

"It's a very small town. The pool of women is probably pretty small. Not even sure there's even a bar." I laugh and head for the door.

"So I have to come to Tulsa every weekend to get my fix, no big deal." He smiles and turns to help the next customer. I just shake my head and go home to get ready for tomorrow. If this all goes well I may only work there a week.

Mom calls when I get inside the front door to tell me it's all set up and they'll be expecting us Friday night. She seems very positive this will work out but I can't help but wonder if it's all too good to be true. It'll get me out of Tulsa where I won't think I see Audrey everywhere and to a place where her memory can quit haunting me. An Audrey free zone. Not sure if that sounds good or bad.

9

I send a quick text to Karlie and Leah knowing that texting is much easier than seeing them in person and trying to keep my know-it-all brothers from figuring it out before I have the chance to tell the girls.

Can u 2 come over? Need 2 talk.

Immediately I get the responses I had hoped for.

B right there.

Yep on my way.

Ok so they're on the way. How in the world do I start this conversation? Are they going to see right through me? Will I chicken out? Holy cow maybe this is a bad idea. What if my brothers come with them? Oh goodness.

Before I can talk myself out of the meeting the doorbell rings. I can tell it's one of the girls because they only ring it once while my annoying brothers ring it again and again until I answer.

Walking up to the door I take a deep breath and exhale as I open it trying to smile like nothing's wrong. Is wrong even the word here? I have wanted to be a mother as long as I can remember. But a single mother was not what I had planned. I can do it yes, but it's still sad to know that I'll be doing it this way.

"Hey ladies. Glad you could come on such short notice. Want some water or tea?"

"Spill it Audrey. What's going on? Did you hear from the doctor today? Is that why we're here?" Karlie asks without taking a breath.

"You're pregnant aren't you?" Leah says and smiles crossing her arms across her stomach.

"Oh my goodness Audrey! Are you pregnant?" Karlie says while jumping up and down screaming.

"How in the world did you figure that out? I didn't even know until the doctor told me!"

"Oh my gosh!!! You are pregnant!!!! Oh my gosh! Oh my gosh! Oh my gosh!" Karlie runs around the room screaming like a mad woman. Shouldn't I be the one acting so erratic? I look at Leah and she's watching Karlie's circus act too smiling in disbelief. When she turns to look at me she gets that crease between her eyebrows that let everyone know she's thinking a little too hard.

"Audrey are you ok? Are you not happy about this news?" She puts her arm around me and pulls me into a hug.

And that's when I lose it and cry like a big baby. I didn't realize I was that upset until now. Before long Karlie realizes what's going on and runs over to join in.

"Audrey I didn't even think to ask you if you were happy about this news. I kinda lost my mind when you said you're going to have a baby. I got a little excited."

"I didn't say anything that's the problem. How in the world did you know before I did?"

"I remember having that exact look on my face when I found out I was pregnant with Shannon. I was so torn because of Lewis' schedule and his drinking. I didn't want to raise a baby alone."

"Oh my goodness Audrey! Prince Charming is the father isn't he?" Karlie says and freezes as she connects all the dots.

"Yes of course he is. What do I do now? I don't even have a way to contact him. I'll be the one in this group raising a baby alone. Alone."

"You will never be raising it alone. You have all of us. Your mother is going to be over the moon to find out you're going to give her another grandchild." Leah says making sure I look right at her when she says those words.

"And your brothers are going to be so excited to have another niece or nephew!"

"Karlie, they're going to hunt Maysen down themselves and kill him."

"Oh. I hadn't thought about that part. They just might do that. Probably a good thing we don't know his phone number. Maybe it wasn't such a bad idea that you didn't get it either time you were with him."

"Now now, no need to rehash that lapse in judgment she had Karlie!" Leah says laughing while nudging me on the arm.

"Thanks you two. You're supposed to be here helping me figure out what I'm going to do and help me come to terms with the idea of being a single mother. I have wanted to be a mother since I was a little girl, but never like this. What did I get myself into?"

"You'll be just fine. There's nothing to worry about with the built in support system you do have. We all love you and will love this baby so much too!"

"Leah I know you're right, I am just really freaked out. And how can I do this to my child? He or she will grow up not knowing his or her father. That's not fair with the wonderful father I grew up with."

"Leah and I understand that Audrey, we just want you to know that we're here if you need anything before and after the baby comes. I have learned so much from Leah and your Mom since I had Aleah. I couldn't have done it without them or my own Mom. Even she would be more than happy to help you out."

"I know. I just feel so terrible knowing that Maysen will be a father and not even know it. Do you think I should try to find him?"

"Didn't we try that while we were in New York? We couldn't find him online anywhere."

"We could go on a little trip to Omaha the next free weekend we all have. I know that Aiden would be glad to have a little bit of time alone with Aleah."

"And Austin can definitely handle the nursery by himself. When is your next long weekend?"

"Actually, it's this weekend. It's the fourth of July. I have Friday off."

"Then it's settled. Where's your laptop? We can get the plans started. I bet the plane tickets might be a little steep with the last minute trip and all but I'm sure we can swing it." Leah smiles and grabs for the laptop I pointed to on the coffee table.

"We can leave Thursday afternoon when you're done with your last class and drive to Tulsa and stay the night. We can get up the next morning and fly out. You could go to the garage you said he worked at and talk to him."

"Oh my gosh Karlie I'm not sure what I would say to him. Hey sorry to bother you but you're going to be a father. I live in

Oklahoma and you live here in Nebraska but I'm sure we could work something out."

"Ok Audrey that does sound terrible."

"Settle down you two. Let's take this one step at a time. I can't leave Friday because of a big delivery coming in but I can leave early Saturday. Looks like there's a flight leaving at 10:30am from Tulsa and it's non-stop to Omaha. They have a room available at that hotel you stayed at when you were there so you'll have no trouble finding the garage." Leah says and reaches for her purse. Once I realize she's pulled out her debit card and paid for the trip I really start to feel anxious. This is final. We're going to Omaha to find Maysen and tell him we're going to be parents.

"I think I'm going to throw up." I sit down on the couch and hang my head in my hands. The room is spinning and I'm not sure if it's the pregnancy or just the thought of facing Maysen.

"What if he's not happy about it and wants me to abort the baby? What if he gets mad and thinks I'm trying to trap him? This could go very wrong. Maybe I'm just better off not telling him." I get up and start pacing the floor.

"Audrey, it's going to be just fine. Karlie and I will be there the whole time. Nothing is going to go wrong."

"Until your brothers find out anyway." Karlie stands to hug me and smiles a very wicked smile.

"That's easy for you to smile about because it isn't your life!" I throw my hands in the air and let out a growl. My brothers are such pains in the butt!

"We have to listen to them every minute that you're not around. It's going to be a nice change to not be on that end of things. You need to tell your mom though." Leah says and hugs me too.

"Thanks girls. You made me feel a little better. I guess

THIRD TIME'S A CHARM

we're going to Omaha Friday. Oh my." I open the door for them to file out of. Each smiles that tender smile that I love to see so much and walks away discussing how exciting it's going to be to have another baby around.

I'm just so unsure about all of this that I couldn't tell you if I'm excited or scared to death. A little of both I think.

Omaha in a few days. Wow this is really happening. Lord help me.

10

"Dude, how far is Hickville? It seems like we've been on the road forever."

"Carter, it's been like twenty minutes. Are you sure you're up to possibly moving there?"

"Moving there and driving there are two different things. If I move there I will already be there Einstein." He says and shakes his head like I said something that was totally off mark.

"Um, ok that made sense. Mom, how far did you say it was?"

"It's about an hour and a half more. It's not a bad drive really. Only takes about two hours to get to the big city if you need to but have the small town feel at home. It's a wonderful place, it really is. You boys will love it. And Carter it's Colvin not Hickville." Mom says and pats Carter on the arm. He smiles at her and decides he needs to keep quiet because she was happy to be going to "Hickville" as he put it.

"Maysen, Aunt Ingrid is expecting us to come straight to their house when we get to town. She's going to have a little lunch ready for us. Then we'll tootle on over to the garage after that to see Uncle Sam."

"Sounds good Mom. I'll be happy to eat anyone else's cooking besides Carter's."

"My frozen entrees are the bomb man what are you talking about?" We all crack up laughing.

"Aunt Ingrid will never allow you two to eat frozen meals again. She and half the ladies in town will probably keep you fed day after day." Mom beams with pride. She really does want this to work out. Not sure if it's for her or Carter and I.

"That sounds like Heaven. What are the ladies like in what did you call it? Calvin?"

"The town is called Colvin. Why's that so hard to remember?"

"Sorry Colvin. What are the ladies like in Colvin?" He smirks at me while raising an eyebrow.

"Carter, there are nice girls that live here in Colvin and they don't need some overly excited young man chasing them around. This isn't the big city we're talking about. They act respectable around here. Please tell me you aren't going to embarrass me."

"Dude, you just got Mom'd. She is right though. Things will probably be different here when it comes to how people act and expect you to act. Don't be dumb like you usually are. We'll be taking over a business that has a reputation. Not the kind you had in Omaha and Tulsa."

"Well, I'm being ganged up on here. I think it's time for me to take a little siesta. Wake me when we're in Hickville." He smiles knowing he said the name wrong again but knew neither Mom nor myself would say anything back. Mom just shakes her head and rolls her eyes. I smile and shrug not knowing what else to say or do.

****

"Hey Mom. Dad here?" I say as I enter my parents' kitchen later that afternoon.

"No, he's gone to town to check on the tractor he has at Sam's. Anything I can help you with?"

"No, I actually wanted to talk to you alone."

"Ok, pull up a seat. I've got some key lime pie left over from last night. Would you like some?"

"Oh my favorite. Please."

"What's going on sweet girl? Classes going ok? I heard you had been feeling bad, better now?"

"Yes, classes are great. The kids are wonderful actually. I just need to tell you something and I really don't know how to tell you."

"Just say it Audrey. You always were one to beat around the bush."

"Well, Mom I'll just say it then." I breathe in deep and exhale hoping courage comes with it.

"You're pregnant aren't you?" Mom says and shocks the stuffing out of me.

"What? How in the world do you all know that but I never had a clue? That is so not fair! When did they tell you?"

"No one told me silly girl. I know you and I know what it's like to be pregnant. I did have four pregnancies you know."

"Mom, I can't believe you already know."

"I didn't know I just had a feeling that's what was wrong with you. The boys said you had been sick and whenever you came for dinner last night you seemed to turn your nose up at everything you normally devour. Didn't take a mother long to figure that out."

"I was clueless Mom. Absolutely clueless. I never in a million years expected to have a baby right now."

"Babies don't always come when we plan them. You were proof of that."

"I know. You've told the 'oops we had Audrey' story a trillion times. At least you were married though. I'm not and now look what I've done. The one time I throw caution to the wind and do something out of the ordinary, it comes back to bite me. Oh Mom. Are you upset with me?"

"Upset with you? You're an adult Audrey. What you choose to do with your life and whom you spend that time with is none of my business. You have always been the responsible one and so what if you had one wild night? You are human and now you're going to be a mother. And I will be a grandmother again. What's there to be upset about?" She walks over and hugs me tightly. This hug from Mom has been my happy place throughout my life thus far.

"Thank you Mom. The girls and I are going to Omaha in a few days to talk to the father. I don't have any other way to get ahold of him. I know how that sounds but I honestly never expected to need to talk to him again. I figured that if it were meant to be it would be."

"Sounds like you're meant to talk to him again." She pats my stomach on her way back to the sink and smiles.

"Oh boy."

****

"Carter, wake up. We're here. Mom's already inside and

you're zonked out in the car. Wake the heck up man." I shake him trying to wake his dead to the world body up.

"I'm up. I'm up. No worries man, I'm up." He jumps up and hits his head on the roof of the car. Idiot. I laugh knowing he's still half asleep. That was video worthy, should have had my phone ready.

"Dangit that hurt. What're you laughing at?" He punches me in the stomach as he gets out of the car.

"You're an idiot. That's what I'm laughing at. Idiot." I punch him back and head to the house. Mom's inside probably giving Aunt Ingrid the lowdown on Carter. Making sure they keep an eye on him and the local ladies I'm sure.

"Aunt Ingrid, this is Carter. Carter, Aunt Ingrid."

"Nice to meet you ma'am. Thank you for having us." He smiles and she swoons. Oh boy. This town has no idea what they've gotten into with Mr. Player of the Day here.

"Okay, let's get these boys fed so they can meet Sam at the garage. I'm so excited for Maysen and Carter to see it. I think they're going to love it. Sam has loved it since he was a boy." Aunt Ingrid smiles like a proud wife should. My gut clenched at that thought because of course my brain conjured up a picture of Audrey beaming like that at me. Wow I am losing it.

"I'm sure we will Aunt Ingrid. What have you got for us to eat? Mom says your casseroles are the best."

"They're the best in the county. Sam has always loved them clear back to the beginning when I brought him one for working on my car before we started dating." She lets out a slow sigh and once again I envision Audrey doing that after we have been married for ages like Sam and Ingrid. Snap out of it man!

"Looks and smells great. We are starved. Right Carter?"

"Most definitely. We drove all the way here for your cooking. And maybe a little garage talk." He smiles and winks at Aunt Ingrid again. I elbow him on my way by towards the table. He just smiles that devilish smile and follows.

"Well boys, I'm going to go get settled in and take a little cat nap. Let me know when you've been to the garage. I'm eager to hear your thoughts." Mom kisses my forehead as if I was a child again and walks to her room in the back of the house. She seems a little tired and I hope that's just from the traveling. But we did only go a couple of hours it's not like we were in the car all day. She did just get out of the hospital so I guess I can stop worrying. Just a little.

"So, Maysen is there a young lady in your life? Carter?"

"No ma'am. We're single." Carter beats me to answering.

"Aunt Ingrid, this is amazing casserole. You'll have to give me the recipe. Seems like something two bachelors could make easily and feed on for a week."

"Oh poppycock. While you're here in town you won't need to cook. You can come by and eat with us or I can bring some things to you."

"Oh ma'am there's no need for that. Maysen loves my frozen dinners that I make." He smiles and winks at me. He's baiting her into offering to cook for us every day. I glare at him and shake my head.

"Well, no more frozen meals for you two handsome men. And with the hours you'll keep at the garage, you won't have time to cook. I should know since I've been married to the current owner for forty-eight years now."

"Wow that's a long time. Congratulations." That really is an accomplishment. If only I could find a woman to be happily married to for that long. And there's the Audrey vision in my head.

71

I'm beginning to think I'm losing my mind with how easily she pops into my head.

"You boys will find your one true loves. Just be patient."

Carter chokes on his food with the "one true loves" remark. I kick him under the table to shut him up. Yes, that was a very female thing to say but I know what she means. I want to meet that one girl I'm meant to be with forever, maybe he's not interested in that but I am. I just won't tell Aunt Ingrid or she might have me set up with every eligible woman in town before sundown.

11

"Hey. Are you ready to go?" Leah asks as I open the door the next morning. Saturday morning, the morning of our flight to Omaha. Ready? Not really. Packed? Yes.

"Let's go then. Have everything you need?" Karlie asks as she picks up my bag and winces when she feels how heavy it is.

"Whatcha got in here? Rocks?"

"I didn't have a clue what I would want to wear when I saw Maysen so I took a few extra things."

"Like your whole closet? You packed more than I do for Aleah and she's almost 5 months old!"

"I know but I couldn't decide. Figured you two would help me decide when the time came."

"Yes we will. Karlie and I will be there every step of the way. You know that right?"

"Yes I do. Thank you two for going with me. I know you have lives of your own."

"You are a part of those lives silly. Let's go. Aleah hasn't woken up yet and I don't want Aiden to call and need me to run over and help once she does. I'll never get out of here."

"Ready or not, here we go." I breathe in and out trying to calm my nerves and keep from throwing up. Goodness I hope this part ends soon.

Have a safe trip girls. Love you all.

"You have the best mother ever!" Leah says as we all get the same text from my Mom.

"She is one of the two best!" Karlie says and smiles.

"Yours is awesome too, yes." We all text Mom back and set off for a trip full of uncertainty.

"What do you think you'll do if he is happy and wants you to stay?"

"Um, I hadn't even thought about that scenario. I was so worried about the negative I never really thought about the positive one."

"Maybe you need to prepare yourself for that too. He didn't sound like the kind of guy to shuck his responsibilities. And if his Mom's as sick as he said, she might love to have a grandbaby around. Especially if she thinks she'll never have one before she dies."

"Oh don't say that Karlie. I would hate to hear that his mother passed away."

"No one would Audrey, but we know first-hand it happens."

"I know Leah but I can't think about that too. I don't know what he's going to think let alone what his Mom's going to. Oh my goodness what am I doing? Take me back home please."

"No ma'am. Tickets are bought and paid for. We are going. You need to do this for you, the baby, and for Maysen. You'll thank us later."

"Or hate you." I shrug and sit back in the seat to relax. Yea right who am I kidding? Relaxing is not something I'm going to be doing any time soon.

****

"Sam, this is Maysen and Carter. Guys, this is Uncle Sam."

"I think they figured that out Ingrid. Goodness woman, you're hovering like an old mother hen. The boys and I will be fine, you can go on now. We need to talk shop. Love you though. See you tonight." He kisses Aunt Ingrid on the cheek and walks her to the car. He even opened the door for her and waited until she drove away to turn and come back inside. Wow people just aren't like that anymore. I could take a page out of his book with….. Audrey. Dangit there I go again.

"Now, do you boys know anything about turning wrenches?"

"Yes sir, we do. We both went to college for automotive and diesel mechanics and both worked at a small garage in Omaha before we moved to Tulsa." I say before Carter can spit something stupid out. He has such a way of opening his mouth and inserting his foot that now isn't the time for that. I'm sure Uncle Sam already thinks we're idiots because we came from the big city.

"Well, let's see what you can do. I have a tractor in the back there that belongs to one of the local ranchers and it needs an overhaul. I've been working on it little by little but I'm getting so old I'm having trouble climbing up and down the ladder."

"Sure, what do you need done? I would be glad to help." Carter says and shocks me that he's beating me to it too.

"Well, I can't get it to idle so if you can diagnose that issue, we'll talk more."

"Yes sir." Carter smiles and takes off his button up shirt leaving the white muscle tee he had on under it. You would think a beautiful woman was in the room with the way he smiled when he threw the shirt to me. I just shake my head and follow Uncle Sam to another vehicle.

"This one here had a transmission overhaul and is about all buttoned back up. You can finish that and I'll go get some paperwork done. You just holler at me when you're all done. But if it gets dark and Ingrid calls for dinner before-hand, I'll holler at you two."

"I don't think he has much faith in our abilities Mayse."

"Well, we'll show him that we can do anything he can." I smile and get to work.

****

"I can't believe I'm back in Omaha. That's the exact restaurant we ate at. Those are the stairs he carried me up after our walk in the park. What have you two gotten me into? I don't think I can do this." I sit down in the nearest lobby chair unable to hold myself up any longer. My emotions are all over the place. On one hand I want so badly to see Maysen again but I'm also so afraid he'll reject me and the baby or be angry.

"You can do this Audrey. Karlie and I are here to help hold you up whenever you need it."

"Let's get our stuff upstairs. I'm sure you'll feel much better once you've freshened up"

"Alright but I've showered here before and I know for a fact they aren't that fabulous. It would take a gold plated shower head and a hundred water jets to make me feel better right now."

"We didn't get the penthouse suite you goober. But I bet we

could arrange that if it'll help!" Karlie giggles. She could make light of anything regardless of the mood. Even if she's the only one that finds it funny, just hearing her giggle does make us all feel even a little better.

"Ha ha. I think I'll take that shower and see you all in a few. Why don't you make yourselves useful and get some room service coming." I smirk and walk into the bathroom fully intending to feel better once the hot water hits me. I have to.

Turning on the faucets and stepping into the hot spray takes me back to the heart break of the last time I took a shower here. Maysen had just left the room after our night together without a word. The last time I saw him.

"The last time I saw your Daddy." I put a hand on my stomach and feel the emotions boiling over again. "Stop it Audrey. You have got to hold it together if for no one other than your unborn child."

I breathe in deep and let the spray soothe the worries away. I will feel better. I will feel better. If only I could convince myself of that.

****

"Well well well. Boys, I have to say you two are hired. That tractor hasn't run in months and you have it purring like a kitten. And that tranny job is done. Wow. You boys know your stuff. I wasn't so sure about city boys knowing anything but I was dead wrong and I apologize."

"No need to apologize. We were ready for an interview of some sort. We didn't figure you would hand over your family business without knowing darn sure that we were the ones for the jobs." I say and shake Uncle Sam's hand as he extends it.

"I will go call AJ who owns that tractor and let him know it's all done. He'll think I'm joking. Probably wanna meet the man who tamed that beast."

"I'd be happy to meet him." Carter says and also shakes Uncle Sam's hand.

"You boys get cleaned up and meet me up front."

Carter and I turn towards the direction he motioned to and saw the sink. A sink that looks as if he had been bathing in grease each day instead of only washing his hands. Cleanliness definitely isn't Uncle Sam's strong suit.

"We'll have our work cut out for us just cleaning up the place."

"I was thinking the same thing. Uncle Sam wasn't a clean freak for sure. That sink looks like it's never been cleaned in the decades he's had the shop open. Aunt Ingrid has probably never been back here either or she would have cleaned it herself." I laugh at the visual that brings to mind.

We dry our hands on the blue towels he has hanging next to the sink and walk towards the office in the front of the shop. As we enter the office we see a tall older man in a straw cowboy hat talking to Uncle Sam. We both smile and await the introductions.

"AJ this here is my nephew Maysen and his friend Carter. They're interested in taking over the repair shop for me. The tall guy here is the one who tamed your beast of a tractor. Gentlemen, this here is AJ and he's one of the best and oldest customers I've got."

"Very nice to meet you sir." Carter and I say in unison.

"Please, call me AJ. And I don't appreciate being called old Sam." He throws his head back with a deep laugh causing the rest of us to laugh too.

"AJ brings all of his ranch vehicles and tractors into the shop year round. He has a few kids too that bring their stuff in. He keeps us fed with all the work he does bring. I have been very grateful for his continued loyalty over the years."

"Ah you hush. Where else would I take my wife's Caddy? We wouldn't trust anyone else with it. I bought her a Cadillac years and years ago once our last was potty trained. She still has it and still drives it every day. Won't let me buy anything new for her."

"So, Uncle Sam says you have a ranch outside of town?" I ask trying to show interest in our possible number one customer. Uncle Sam was trying to hint that this is the man that keeps the lights on in this place.

"The 6AB Ranch. We have about 500 acres northeast of town. You should come out one of these days and take a tour. My middle son takes care of the breeding program while I deal with the rest of it."

"How many kids do you have?"

"Three boys and a girl. Either of you married and or have kids?"

"No. Neither of us have any ball and chain." Carter spits out hoping for a laugh but gets a stern look from AJ and Uncle Sam.

"Nothing wrong with the ball and chain. Beats cooking your own dinner and doing your own laundry." AJ laughs again which this time we all laugh too because the tension was so high from Carter's failed attempt at humor.

"Well, I'm going to call Aiden right now and have him bring one of the hands to town so we can get that tractor home. Send me a bill Sam. I will see you boys around. Let me know if there's anything I can do to help your decision of buying or not. It's a good, solid place. Couldn't go wrong." He slaps Uncle Sam on the back and walks out the front door.

"You boys passed yet another test. He's a hard nut to crack when it comes to his business sense. He's one of my oldest friends and customers. You get his seal of approval, you get the town's. Good job."

"Thank you sir, but we just did what we know. We both enjoy working on cars and things. It's not work to us." Carter says and looks to me for agreement. I nod my head and smile at Uncle Sam.

"I have a few calls to make. If you boys wanna go lock up the garage doors and meet me at the house we'll sit down at the table and talk business."

"That works. See you there." I say and head back into the shop area shutting both overhead doors and locking them.

Walking out the front door after making sure the shop is secure; we see that another two gentlemen have joined AJ outside with the tractor. AJ sees us exit the building and calls us over.

"Hey boys, come on over here and meet my son. Aiden, this is Maysen and Carter. They're here to talk to Sam about taking over the repair shop. This one's the one who fixed the tractor." He motions toward Carter who just nods.

"Nice to meet you guys. Sam has been such an asset to have. He always knows what's wrong and just how to get the job done. Hope we can continue to get the same from you guys if you do take over."

"Yes sir. We're seriously considering relocating to Colvin and doing just that. We would appreciate the continued loyalty." I say and shake Aiden's hand before Carter can.

"Sam always made it easy. Just tell him what was wrong and it would come back fixed. So, where you guys from?"

"Tulsa. We're down for the weekend to check things out."

"Big city boys huh? This is a pretty small town compared to Tulsa. You sure you won't get bored?"

"Nah, we plan on being very busy with the repair shop if we do make that decision. Plus it's only two hours to the city if we need to get out."

"True. This place really is a great place to live. You married?"

"No. You?" I ask seriously wanting to know this answer. Why would it matter to me if this man is married or not? Maybe if he can find a great woman here there's hope for Carter and I.

"Yes. Been married a while and have a six month old little girl too."

"Well congrats, that's awesome. One of these days I hope to have that too. Someday."

"It's slim picking around here. That's one drawback."

"I bet. We aren't looking for a woman here, so I think we'll be good."

"For a while." He laughs.

"Carter here is the typical ladies' man, complete opposite of me."

"I can't help it if the ladies just love me."

"I used to be that man before Karlie came back from New York."

"Old ball and chain got ya did it?"

"For sure. Wouldn't trade it for the world though. Speaking of, my wife is gone this weekend with the girls so I better get back and pick up the munchkin from Mom's. You guys would make a great addition to Colvin. You should stick around. Call me if you want a tour and maybe have a beer." He walks to a black dually pickup and hops inside.

Watching the stocky cowboy pull away makes me feel even better about this move and new opportunity. This really could work and might be just what we've been waiting for.

****

"Okay, we'll be right here if you need us. Walk in there and ask for him by name. You can do it." Leah says and pushes me towards the door to the repair shop I knew Maysen worked at.

Well here goes.

"Hello there! Did I win the lottery today or what? Three gorgeous females walk into my life at one time. Wow. What can I do for you?" A slimy older gentleman greets us once we get inside the door.

"Um, we need to see Maysen Correli. I have a matter I need to take up with him."

"What do you need that loser for? He's worthless and not here anymore."

"What do you mean not here anymore? Did he get fired?" Karlie asks.

"No gorgeous, he and his equally worthless friend quit and I really don't know where they went. Or care."

"Do you have any way to get in contact with them? It's very important that we talk to Maysen" Leah says stepping forward.

"Nope. You're out of luck. I can do anything for you that Maysen could." He grins a creepy grin which makes our skin crawl.

"No thank you. I think I'll try to find Maysen. Thank you for your time." I say and usher the girls out the door as fast as my feet will take me.

"Oh my goodness that man was so creepy. I think I need a

shower to wash off the way he looked at me. Yuck." Karlie says and shivers. Leah and I both look at her and laugh in agreement.

"He was so gross. All bald and stinky. Wow."

"Yes, but now what do we do? We came all the way here to talk to Maysen and now he's not here with no way to contact him." I say feeling defeated.

"Honey, I think you have done all you can do. This baby is going to be raised by a wonderful mother and family. Like I said before, if it's meant to be with him it will be." Leah says and hugs me tightly sensing that I was about to fall apart again.

"Let's go home. We can change our flights and leave this place behind for good this time. Sound good Audrey?"

"Karlie, you're right. Let's go get our stuff and go home. I just need to be home."

12

"I can't believe he moved. How do I ever find him now?" I say to the girls and look out the airplane window as we take off from Omaha. What a wasted trip.

"Audrey, you tried. Now you just move forward and be the best mommy you can be." Leah reaches over and squeezes my hand.

"You'll be fine. You have all of us and don't need him. That baby you're carrying will be just fine too. Surrounded by lots of love and support." Karlie joins in.

"Thanks girls. I couldn't have done any of this without you two. I know you guys will be around if I need you it's just not the outcome of this trip that I was praying for."

"We know and we understand. Step by step." Karlie leans her head back to rest. "I need to get a little nap in before Miss Aleah has me up all night. You should enjoy your sleep while you can."

We all laugh and relax back into our seats for the short flight back to Tulsa. My mind wanders back to the two times I've happened upon Maysen and wonder if I'll have another one. It's very possible that I may never see him again. Will my baby grow up not knowing its father? That breaks my heart. The one time I throw caution to the wind and it ends up affecting someone else's life too. I am so not okay with this. But what can I do?

****

"Well, what do you think of the garage? Something you might want to take on?" My mother asks when we walk in the door at Aunt Ingrid's. Her face shows all the hope she's holding onto that this deal will work out and we'll both move here to Colvin.

"You know, it might actually work Ma. We met a couple of the customers today and they seemed great to work with and willing to work with us. I'm not sure one time in there is enough though."

"Maysen, this is a big decision and you can't make it lightly. It's not just your livelihood on the line but also Uncle Sam's reputation."

"Mom, I know that believe me. It's weighing heavy on my mind. I'm going to go shower so I can drive Carter back to Tulsa."

"He's going back today?"

"Yeah, he got called into work the bar tonight. I'm taking him but I'll be back."

****

Landing in Tulsa didn't change the way the day has been going. Karlie borrowed her mom's car and about a mile from the airport it broke down.

"Austin thanks for coming to pick us up but are you seriously going to leave my Mom's car sitting here alongside the road?" Karlie asks with the worry apparent in her voice.

"Dad called Sam and he'll come pick it up with the tow

truck. No worries. He's probably already on his way too." Austin says and kisses Leah on the forehead as he reaches for her bag.

"You're sure it'll be ok here babe?" Leah asks and reaches for my bag. I shoot her a dirty look knowing she's afraid to let me pick up my bag because of the pregnancy. I'm not ready for my nosy brothers to know about the baby. I have a feeling it's not going to be long before their significant others spill the beans though.

"Yes. Now, how was the trip? Weren't you supposed to come home on Sunday?"

"Babe, let's just get everyone home. We're tired and Karlie's really missing Aleah."

"Got it." He looks at me with a look of inquisition on his face but knows better than to ask. Yep, my brothers will know by day's end. Wonderful.

****

"Hey Maysen, I'm needing to go to Tulsa to pick up a car for AJ. I guess his daughter and daughters in law broke down a mile or so from the airport. We can take Carter home at the same time. Then you can see another side of the customer service the garage offers to the good customers." Uncle Sam smiles and heads out the front door.

I guess we're going to Tulsa in a tow truck. Sounds fun. Reminds me of being on call in Omaha though. That part I'm not excited about inheriting with the garage.

"So, are we picking up the ladies too?" Carter asks when we're headed out of Colvin.

"Nope. Austin already went to get them. He's another son of AJ's. He owns the Stampley's Nursery outside of town with his fiancé."

"How many of them are there?"

"They are off limits Carter. Don't answer that Uncle Sam." I shoot Carter a glare and smile at Uncle Sam. I'm not sure Carter's heart is in this whole thing for the right reasons. He's thinking of another group of women to sleep with while I'm thinking of my future and being near my mother.

"So, Uncle Sam do you think we could work for you for a couple of weeks to get a real feel for the business before we make a big leap?"

"I was thinking the same thing. You two did great things today but that's just a little bit of time. How soon could you come back?"

"I can come back right now and just call the dealership. I started this week but wasn't too interested in it and I really don't think they were that interested in me."

"Carter? When can you come to work?" Uncle Sam asks.

"I'm not sure. I'll get back to you." He shrugs and turns to his ever buzzing cell phone.

"I'll grab some of my stuff at the house when we drop Carter off."

"Then we'll go get the girls' car and head home." Uncle Sam says and I can see a hint of satisfaction in his voice. Maybe he wants this take over more than I thought he did. I just wish I knew what Carter was thinking. I take out my own cell phone and text him. I know he'll answer that way since he's ALWAYS on it.

Dude, you not into this anymore? Need to know.

I hear his phone buzz as he receives my text and we catch eyes when he looks up. I can see the uncertainty then. I had no idea he was so on the fence about it.

Idk man. That town is so small. I really don't know.

I read his text to me and I'm really not surprised.

K. *Let me know ASAP.*

I text a quick reply and look out the window. I feel a great deal of peace about this move and a little excitement too. I could really use the change. And I'll love being close to Mom full time.

****

Home Sweet Home. That might be what the wreath says on the front door but right now it seems lonely. I guess a part of me was hoping to see Maysen and have that happily ever after. A part of me? Who am I kidding? I was praying with my whole being that we would have that.

Now that I'm home alone without him, how do I move on with a new baby? As I get my stuff set down I can hear someone moving in behind me. I turn and melt as soon as I see my mother's sweet smiling face on the other side of the glass door.

When I walk towards the door and open it I hear her say, "Oh honey I can tell by your face things didn't go so well?"

I shake my head and step into her outstretched arms and begin to cry like I've never cried before. Crying for the fairy tale I always wanted and won't have. Crying for the father figure I wanted this baby to have. Crying for the loving and devoted husband I desperately wanted for myself. With all these darn hormones I'm crying for every little thing I can think of.

****

"You know, AJ has quite the looker for a daughter. Never been married, smart as a whip and a big sweetheart too. Maybe we should introduce the two of you if you decide to stay."

"Uncle Sam, I really can't deal with a girlfriend and all the issues that come along with one right now. This move and job will be enough to handle. Thanks but no thanks." My mind flashes to

Audrey sitting across from me at dinner in that dress. Now if that woman walked in my door I would be more than happy to be introduced.

"I understand. Women can be nothing but a distraction sometimes. That is until you find that one you're a sucker for. Then it's all over but the cryin'. When you do find your Ingrid, you'll have a change of heart."

"Someday I'm sure things will change but right now I have to stay focused on the repair shop."

"You sound like you've made up your mind already."

"I'm leaning towards yes more and more." I smile and look out the window again watching the scenery change from Tulsa to the middle of nowhere the closer we come to Colvin.

I think the slow lifestyle would be a much needed change. I can start a new chapter with new people and be close by for Mom.

And hopefully be too busy to let that blond keep popping into my head. And heart. Dangit! There's no chance of ever seeing her again so why can't I forget her? Get a grip Maysen.

13

"Amelia, there's a new guy taking over Sam's Garage. He's actually Sam's nephew. Ingrid's sister, Martha's boy. Pretty boy type but he knows his stuff it seems. Sam's excited to get him in there so he can finally retire. It's about time he does that. Ingrid's been nagging him for years to retire." I can hear Dad say when he walks into the kitchen the next morning.

"That is wonderful to hear. I'll have to drop by and see Ingrid and Martha sometime this week. He's a handsome fellow huh? Maybe we should introduce him to Audrey."

"Mom no. I do not need a fix up. Especially now." I growl, turn around and stomp towards the door. I do not need my parents setting me up with a man just because I'm pregnant. But as I think of going on a date with a man I feel like I would be cheating on Maysen. I can't imagine another man touching me either. I have lost it now for sure. Get a grip on yourself Audrey! You're going to be a mother in a few months. I need to worry about the baby and getting things ready not worrying about men. Ugh!

****

"Ready for your first day on the job?" Uncle Sam asks me

as we head out the door Monday morning and towards the shop.

"You know, I'm very ready. What's on the agenda?"

"First we need to get on Ella Mae Doone's car. It needs diagnosed first. I'll let you do that while I get the rest of the day scheduled."

"I can do that. Um, which one's her car?"

"The one we picked up in Tulsa for AJ. Ella Mae is Aiden's mother in law."

"Ah I see. This town is small; I need to remember that fact." I smile and walk away to get started. Everyone seems to know or be related to everyone here.

After working on the little blue car that belongs to one of the shop's best customers, I walk back up to the office where Uncle Sam said he would be. As I am ready to enter the office door something else grabs my attention.

Just outside the door I see a white car pull up and a dark haired young lady get out of the passenger side. As I see her say something to the driver and laugh, I glance at the driver and my heart stops. Before I can get my wits about me the car drives away. I have to shake my head and open and close my eyes a few times to come back to reality. I could have sworn I just saw Audrey in the driver's seat of that car. I am really losing it if I'm hallucinating her being around here now too.

Before I can get too into what I'm feeling the brunette walks into the shop and straight for the office door I'm currently stopped in front of.

"Hi, I'm here to see Sam." She says and all I can do is step aside and let her enter his office.

"Hey Karlie, you here to check on your Mama's car? I think it's about done. Isn't it son?"

"Um, yes sir. I was just coming up to let you know it was done. It was the fuel pump. It's good to go and parked out front." I hand the lady the keys and walk out the door knowing I just looked like a total dummy.

"Maysen, you did a great job on Karlie's mom's car. She's Aiden's wife." Uncle Sam finds me a few minutes later in the back of the shop cleaning up my mess.

"Thank you. It was nothing. So, that was Aiden's wife huh? No wonder he's okay with the old ball and chain." I smile and wink at Uncle Sam.

"Yeah, she's a beauty for sure." And he walks away leaving me to continue on with the scheduled vehicles. I am still pretty shook up over the hallucination of Audrey in that car though. This is what it's come to? It was bad enough when I thought about her all the time, now I'm seeing her too. Great.

****

"All set? I bet your mom's relieved to have her car back." I ask Karlie as she gets into my car again after picking up and dropping off her mom's car.

"Yes, thanks for the ride over there and for picking me up now."

"Sure. I was headed to town anyway so it's all good. You're not in a hurry to get home are you? I need to go get groceries for Mom."

"Nope. Aiden has Aleah and I'm not sure she's feeling well. She might be teething. I need to get some of that gel for the gums in case she is."

"That doesn't sound fun. I need to fill my prescription for prenatal vitamins too so let's head for the pharmacy first."

"Works for me. Man, your Dad was right about the guy

92

working for Sam now. Holy buckets he's hot. If I wasn't married I might have stuck around to stare and drool."

"That good huh?"

"Yes and seemed really nice too but shy. Like someone else I know." She smiles and wiggles her eye brows at me.

"I don't want set up Karlie. I've already said that to all of you. No match making please."

"Got it but he really was hot with a capital H."

I shake my head and roll my eyes knowing he probably was hot but I really don't need set up. If only they would realize I was serious.

"So, when's the next doctor appointment? You'll get to see the baby then right? And hear the heartbeat?"

"Yes. It's tomorrow actually. I'm getting really excited."

"Kinda? I'm ecstatic! Can I go with you?"

"Sure. Leah and Mom had asked me too. It's at 3 o'clock. Just meet me there. I'm going straight from class."

"I'll catch a ride with Leah. You'll get to see your little one for the first time and then it'll be more real for you. I promise."

"I know it will, still wish Maysen were here to experience it with me. I know that's crazy since I only saw him twice but I feel bad that he's out there somewhere missing out on his child's development."

"Audrey you really can't think about that. You went to Omaha to find him but he was gone. There's nothing else you can do but take the best care of yourself and this baby."

"I know. I'm so emotional right now and I can't think straight, it's ridiculous." I roll my eyes and she giggles knowing exactly what I'm talking about.

"Get used to it. The baby takes over your body and it's never the same again. I'd give anything to be able to hold my pee in longer than two seconds!" We both laugh and head into the pharmacy.

I hear my phone sing the tone I had set for my best friend Tracey. But she's in rehab and not in town. I haven't heard from her in a very long time. I look up for Karlie but she's left me and starting her shopping farther down the aisle.

"Hello?"

"Audrey? It's Tracey. I hope it's okay that I'm calling."

"Of course it is! How're you doing?"

"I'm doing great actually. I'm getting out of here tomorrow morning. I was hoping I could come see you sometime? Or have you not forgiven me yet? I would totally understand if you haven't."

"Oh Tracey, I forgave you before it happened. You've been my best friend for so long I wouldn't know what to do without you. Please come see me whenever you come to town."

"Are you sure? I wouldn't want to hurt anyone. I've done that enough."

"No no no. I would be so happy to see you. Please come see me. I've thought about you every single day but we were told we couldn't contact you. I am so pleased to know you're doing so well!"

"I'll call you when I know a little more about when I'll be up that way."

"Deal. I can't wait to see you. Take care and congrats!"

"Ok bye my friend. See you soon."

I hang up my phone and smile because she sounds so much more like the old Tracey. She got mixed up with some bad people and bad stuff. We got her into rehab and she's been there for a long time. Seems like forever without her. I am so happy she's going to be released and doing so well. I can't wait to see her.

"Hey what's got you smiling so big? Baby move for the first time?"

"No, I just got a call from Tracey. She's being released tomorrow and wanted to know if she could come see me."

"Oh that's so great to hear. I'm glad she's doing better."

"Are you? She's afraid she'll upset people if she comes back to town after what happened."

"Of course she's welcome back here. We all know she was going through such a hard time. Heroine is a nasty thing and to know she got healthy is a very big deal."

"You are so amazing Karlie. You know that? She almost came between you and Aiden but you're still supportive. Amazing."

"Hey, it's not a big deal. He married me remember? And had the baby with me. Nothing for me to be upset about."

"Let's get going. I need to help Mom fix dinner tonight."

****

"Hey Maysen, I was looking for you." I wheel out from under the pickup I'm working under and see Aiden standing next to me.

"What for? Did the tractor break down again?"

"No nothing like that. I wanted to invite you out to our house for dinner tonight."

"I would love to but my Mom's cooking tonight. She's

95

finally feeling better and wants to cook for us. I could do a drink after if you're interested."

"A drink would be good."

"When and where?"

"There's only one place in town you can get a beer. It's a little place around the corner from here. Does eight work for you?"

"That's perfect. I'll catch ya then."

"See you then." I watch him walk away and feel happy to know that I have my first friend here in Colvin.

14

"Hey Leah, what're you doing here? Don't you and Austin have plans?" I ask as I open the door for her to come in.

"Nope. He went with Aiden to town to meet the new guy at the repair shop for a beer. Aiden seems to really like him for some reason. Austin wanted to go check him out."

"Men. They seem to be chummy pretty fast. Well, I don't really know how long the new guy's been here. Dad and Karlie swear he's hot. Well, Dad didn't say hot!" We both laugh.

"So, when do you have the ultrasound?"

"Tomorrow morning at ten; I'm getting excited."

"Your Mother is over the moon because you're letting her go with you. And I can't wait to do the flowers for your baby shower. You will have one right?"

"I know she's excited. She won't stop confirming the time with me. I don't know if she's afraid I'll change my mind or what. She's kinda driving me nuts about it. And yes of course I'll let you two throw me a baby shower."

"Better get used to it. We're all very excited about the baby!"

"You're really starting to get a bump. You're the cutest pregnant blonde I have ever seen!"

"Nice way to not discriminate against Karlie! You're so wise Leah!" I pat her on the shoulder and laugh.

"Well, in this big of a family it's hard to tell everyone the same thing at the same time. Everyone is always going in different directions. I can't even imagine how your parents felt when you were all growing up!"

"I know. I think this baby's the only one in my future. I can't imagine four."

"Three boys to boot!"

"Wanna watch a movie until Austin gets home? I have the newest one we talked about the other day."

"It's a date. I'll get the popcorn."

****

"Hey man, glad you could make it. This is my older brother Austin. This is the guy from the garage I've been telling you about. What'll you have?"

"Nice to meet you Austin, I'll have whatever's on tap."

"Nice to finally meet the mechanic God that Aiden's been bragging about. Oh and thanks for helping Sam get Ella Mae's car from Tulsa. Those girls find trouble wherever they go."

"It was no problem. I just fix them, no special powers involved."

"The way Aiden has talked about you you'd think you were a super hero."

"Shut up man. He's going to think I want to ditch my wife for him." Aiden says slapping me on the back as I take the first drink of my beer.

"Nah, we're good. I've seen your wife and no man would turn away from a woman that looks like her. Congrats man."

"She is great isn't she? I take it she picked up her mom's car today?"

"Yes. Are you married too Austin?"

"Not yet. We haven't set a date yet."

"You ever heard of Leah Frankle?"

"The model? The one in all the expensive purse and perfume ads?"

"That's the one. She's not doing that anymore though. She and I own the nursery here in town."

"Nice. I thought she was married to a baseball player though? I take it not anymore?"

I see Austin and Aiden freeze and try to figure out how to answer so I say, "Hey sorry for prying. None of my business. Next subject."

"Nah, it's ok just don't know where to begin. No, they're not married anymore. I guess that's the short answer."

"Good enough for me. So, you two are gonna get hitched too huh?"

"Yes. I asked her to marry me a while back. We've been so busy with the nursery and remodeling her Grandparents'' old house we haven't had time to even talk about a date, let alone the whole wedding. We're not in a big hurry, our family on the other hand, are."

"I can understand that. I'm taking one day at a time. Thankful for the opportunity to start this new venture and thankful for new friends. Cheers."

We clink our drinks together and then all get silent.

"Well, Sam tells me you have a big ranch outside of town?"

"Yep, the 6AB Ranch. You should come out sometime. Ever ridden a horse?"

"Um can't say that I have. I could come out to watch though. Not sure my pride is sound enough for horse riding lessons at my age."

"Deal. We have a lot going on most of the time. Austin here isn't around the ranch much but I'm always there. Karlie and I live not far from the main homestead."

"Nice. So, there's four of you right, three boys and a girl?"

"Yep, there's a brother older than me and our baby sister. Of course Aiden's wife Karlie and my fiancée Leah now too."

"Only you two are married or close to it?"

"You've seen this town. It's small and not much to choose from."

"Our older brother lives in the big city and as far as we know doesn't have time for the ladies. And our sister, well we thought she didn't have a man but now she's been knocked up by some jerk that left town and never looked back."

"Wow, that's rough. No man should do that to a woman or child."

"Do you have any siblings?"

"Nope. Just Mom and I. Dad left before I was born. Now we have Aunt Ingrid and Uncle Sam around."

"They're great people. Welcome to town, we're glad you're here."

"Thanks, I'm beginning to like it here too. Starting to kinda feel like home."

"Don't look now but there's lady down there with her eyes all over you."

"Ah no thanks. I have enough on my plate right now. No time for a woman."

"Still getting over someone are you?"

"That obvious huh? I can't quit thinking about her or seeing her everywhere. That's the main reason I moved here. Simpler life and new start. Mom really needs me right now too. No time for a woman. None."

"That's what I thought too until Karlie came back. When you find the right one you'll change your mind."

"That seems to be the consensus. Thanks for the company guys but I need to get home. Take care."

"We need to get back too. I left Leah at the ranch so I'm sure we're staying at your house tonight man."

"I'm sure the girls are all watching chick flicks. See ya."

****

"Ok well I had better go now and let you get some rest. I think we're staying with Aiden and Karlie tonight unless Austin decides he wants to drive home. See you at breakfast, maybe."

"See you then. Love you. Thanks for the company."

"Maybe next time we'll go with the guys and find you a man."

"No thank you. Not at the bar for sure."

"Deal. Talk soon." She kisses my cheek and walks away into the dark night.

I feel a small twitch of jealousy that she has my brother to go home to. Even if it's just my other brother's house. She still has someone who loves her and will never leave her. But with what she has been through, it makes my problems seem minuscule. I need to quit feeling sorry for myself. Enough. No more. Yeah right if only it were that easy. Ugh!

****

"Hey Ma, what're you doing awake? It's late. You need your rest."

"Did you have a good time son?"

"Yes it was good. Why are you awake?"

"I wanted to hear about your night. Did you meet a nice young lady?"

"No Ma, I had a few beers with the Blake boys Austin and Aiden."

"Their sister is really pretty and sweet. Maybe they can introduce you."

"No Ma. I'm good. You need to go to bed."

"You need to go find the girl that's stolen your heart Maysen."

"What are you talking about Ma?"

"I can tell by the way you're shutting yourself off that you're hiding from something or someone."

"I just went and had a few drinks with some new friends.

How am I hiding?"

"You moved to Tulsa so quickly and then here. That tells me there was something in Omaha that spooked you and sent you home. Who is she?"

"Ma, I only saw her twice. I have no way of finding her now either. I was foolish enough twice to not get her number."

"Fate brought you two together twice?"

"I guess you could call it that. Once in Tulsa when you were in the hospital and once in Omaha when she was there for a teaching convention. Her car broke down and I towed it to the garage."

"Fate works in mysterious ways my son. You will see her again, you're meant to be together. I just know it."

"You need to rest Ma, you're delirious. Love you."

"Goodnight Maysen. See you tomorrow. You need to get some rest too. Love you."

With that sentiment we both walk to our bedrooms for hopefully a good night's sleep. But as I'm readying for bed, I can't help hearing Mom's comments about fate. It had brought Audrey and I together twice. Could it do it again or would I be an even bigger fool to think it would?

****

Lying here in bed tonight I can't seem to fall asleep. I keep running through my head the last time I stumbled upon Maysen. I had thought it was something that would never happen again but it did. Could we really see each other again?

Of course not you idiot. He's moved and God only knows where to. I need to move on and forget about him. I owe it to both us and the baby to move on and do whatever I can to make this baby feel loved. Loved without a father. But I will always love it and be here. That this baby can count on. I don't need a man's help raising my child. Not at all.

15

Today's the day I get to see my baby for the first time, see his/her little legs and arms. Oh and hear it's heartbeat! I am so excited I can barely stand sitting through this morning's lessons. "Ok kids, I'll be gone for a while but Mrs. Marlin will be in to be your sub while I'm gone."

"Where are you going Miss Blake? You're not leaving for good are you?"

"No Whitney, I'm not. I just have a doctor's appointment today. I'll bring you back a picture of the baby. Deal?"

"Yes! We can't wait to see if it's a boy or a girl! Will you tell us today?"

"If the doctors tell me I'll tell you. Ok?" I start to put my suit coat back on as Mrs. Marlin comes into my classroom. "They're all ready for reading time and then recess. I'll be back as soon as I can."

"Today's the day isn't it?"

"Yes it is. Take care of these kids for me. I'll be back soon. Bye kids. Be good for Mrs. Marlin." I wink at my sub and walk out feeling as if I'm a child on Christmas again.

Just as I get to the front doors of the school I can see a swarm of people standing just outside of them. I open the doors expecting to find strangers huddled around out there, but instead it's people I know and love very much.

"What are all of you doing here?" It was my Mom, Dad, Austin, Leah, Aiden, Karlie, and even Aleah.

"We couldn't wait to see the newest Blake member so we're all going to go with you."

I must have had a horrified look on my face because my Dad says, "We'll all be in the waiting room Dear. Only Mama's going in with you don't worry."

Everyone laughs and I, myself, laugh with all my being for the first time in a long time. It feels good to be happy and ready for whatever is to come in my future.

"Well, let's go then!" And we all pile into our cars and pickups heading to the clinic. We probably look like a Blake family parade. I smile at that thought and feel butterflies in my stomach. I put my hand on my stomach and Mom who's riding with me sees.

"Did you feel the baby move?"

"I'm not sure it was weird and hard to describe."

"Like little butterflies fluttering around?"

"Exactly like that. It was my baby?"

"I bet so. That feeling will get so much stronger as the baby grows. Your little bump may look like a cantaloupe now but soon when it's a watermelon you'll start seeing the movement from the outside too."

"I can't wait Mom. Thank you for coming with me."

"Anything." We get out at the clinic and head inside to see

my baby.

****

This week is slipping by and I'm loving every minute of it. I love being busy and not having a sleaze ball around like in Omaha. I can work on what I want when I want not worrying about people complaining all the time about the owner. I am the owner. Well, once it's all official anyway. Uncle Sam has been leaving me be and letting me start taking things over as if I were the owner.

"Maysen, do you think you could handle the garage for a week or so? Your Aunt would like to go on a little vacation. And since I've owned the garage we've never really done that."

"Of course. That would be a good test to make both of our decisions. When are you leaving?"

"We were thinking about tomorrow if that'll work for you."

"That works just fine. We have the schedule done and I can help anyone else that does come in. The garage will be just fine. Have fun and relax. I'm sure you haven't done that for a while."

"No. It's been so nice not having it all riding on my shoulders since you came. I really think this is going to work Maysen. I thank you for your interest. I'm happy to keep it in the family too."

"I'm the one thankful for the opportunity. Go, go on vacation. Things will be just fine while you're gone."

"You're going to be your Aunt's hero. You do know that don't ya? She's going to be smothering you with food when we get back."

"That's nice but I need to find a place of my own. Especially if I plan on staying."

"You may need privacy someday." He wiggles his

eyebrows at me and walks away whistling. I think that poor man has worked so hard over the years that he feels as light as a feather.

Privacy isn't something I'm going to need any time soon. I'll need somewhere quiet though away from the family. Family is a good thing, just not around 24/7. My own space is one thing I miss about Omaha. And Carter. I wonder what he's up to.

"Hey man, what's up? Yeah I think I'm going to. Sure you don't want a job? Of course I would. Things have been great. Yes. No women. You saw this place. Nope. My Aunt and Uncle are going on some week vacation tomorrow so I'll have a trial run at doing the whole owner thing by myself. Yeah, I'm sure it'll be fine. What could go wrong? No, don't answer that. Yes, you're always welcome. I know I need to start looking. I think I'll go call an agent right now. Take care. See ya soon. Don't party too hard man. Bye."

I shake my head at the image of Carter partying it up with all the women he has and feel so lucky to not be there. Partying never was my thing. I would rather be home than out doing something wild. How Carter and I have gotten along so well all these years is beyond me. He's a great guy, just needs to grow up. I don't see him doing that any time soon though.

"Hey Aiden, it's Maysen at Sam's." I dial the number listed on the last work order we had for the 6AB.

"Hey man, what's up?"

"I was hoping I could get the name and number of a good realtor here. Anyone in town do that sort of thing?"

"You need a place to rent or buy?"

"Rent for now. At least until we figure out for sure if I buy the garage or not."

"Ah I see. Well, to be honest with you I don't think there's anywhere for rent right now but Austin does still have his little house. Since he and Leah got all hot and heavy he's been staying with her. I can call and see what he plans on doing with it."

"That would be awesome. Thanks. Just let me know if he wants to rent it or whatever. If not it's no big deal either. I can always keep crashing at my Aunt and Uncle's."

"I'm sure you can but every man needs his own space. Right?"

"Yes for sure. Thanks again. Bye."

"I'll get back with you."

"Appreciate it." Hanging up the phone I look down at it for a few seconds. People here are so nice. He didn't bat an eye when I asked for his help. Both the boys and their dad seem to be great men.

****

"Who was that? Your new best friend?" I ask Aiden after he gets off the phone. We're all sitting in the waiting room and I'm thankful there isn't anyone else here because there aren't many chairs left.

"The guy from the garage, if you must know. He's looking for somewhere to rent. Austin, what're you gonna do with your house?"

"He could rent it. I just need to get the rest of my junk out. Most of it's already at Leah's so it wouldn't take but a couple of hours."

"Great, I'll let him know. Sis, are you sure you don't want us all in there with you?"

"Oh my goodness no. I completely appreciate you all coming but I don't expect you to stay. If you need to go, by all means, go."

"You sure? Let's go Austin." Aiden says while getting up and kissing his wife and child both on the forehead.

"Love you sis." They say in unison walking out the clinic doors. I look over at Dad and he's shaking his head at the sight of his sons hightailing it out of the women's clinic.

"Cowards." He says and kisses Mom on the cheek. He also stands up and walks away.

"Wow, tough men in this family." Leah says with so much humor in her voice that we all break out laughing too.

"Audrey Blake?" We hear the nurse call from the hallway. I turn to Mom and she smiles which tames the nerves I suddenly got.

"That's you baby girl. Let's go see your baby now." She stands up, grabs ahold of my hands and pulls me up too.

I look over at Leah, Karlie and my niece. "You don't have to stay either. We can meet you at Sally's when we're done here."

"Okay if Aleah gets cranky we'll do just that. Good luck! Can't wait to see the pictures of our niece or nephew!"

I turn and walk with Mom towards the smiling nurse. She's the same one who took me back the day I found out I was pregnant. I wonder to myself if she remembers me and my fainting spell I had. That was embarrassing so I pray she doesn't.

"How're you feeling Audrey?" She asks breaking me out of my own mind. Yep, she remembers.

"Sick. I've had terrible morning sickness. It's been a little better the past couple of days though."

"You're in the second trimester so it should be getting better. For the most part it should be over."

"Goodness I hope so."

"Your stomach is measuring right where it should be. I can feel the baby's head right here. Have you felt it moving around at all?"

"I just started to feel it today actually."

"Amazing feeling, isn't it?"

"Very. We're doing an ultrasound today right? I am so anxious to see the baby."

"Yes, let's go to the other room now and the tech will be there in a few minutes. Everything looks great on our end."

"Thank you so much." Mom and I veer off left towards the new room that has all ultrasound machines in it. I feel a wave of excitement come over me and it takes all the energy I have not to jump up and down.

"Go ahead and lay down, she'll be right with you."

"Thank you."

After what seemed like a million minutes later, another lady in scrubs came into the room. She turns on the machine and grabs a bottle of something that I can't quite make out.

"Miss Blake I need you to lie down on your back and roll your waistband down and pull the shirt up. This is going to be cold, just warning you."

As she squeezes the jelly like liquid onto my stomach, she reaches for the machine that's going to show me my baby inside my stomach.

"There's the head, the legs and the arms. Baby is looking at us today. Can you see the heart beating there inside the chest cavity?"

"Yes oh my goodness Mom! Look, it's a real baby!" I start to cry seeing the child I'm carrying moving around.

"That's your little baby in there Audrey. I am so happy for you." Mom kisses my hand and we both turn back to the screen.

"Would you like to know what gender the baby is Miss Blake?"

I look at Mom and she nods at me. I take a deep breath and look back at the nurse.

"Yes please. Can you tell?"

"Yes I can. Are you sure you want to know if you're having a boy or a girl?"

"Yes please." I turn towards the monitor again awaiting the news of my baby's gender.

"It's a boy Miss Blake. You're going to have a little boy."

I scream and cry. My Mom is screaming and crying. We must look like totals idiots crying and blubbering on like this.

"A baby boy. I'm going to have a son. I'm going to have a son." I put both of my hands on my stomach and say a little prayer that I'm going to be able to protect and raise this child the way he deserves.

"You can get composed again and I'll get these pictures printed off for you of your son."

"Ok thank you."

"A grandson. I'm going to have a granddaughter and a grandson. I love you kids so much." Mom starts to tear up again but I throw my arms around her and cry myself before she has the chance to.

"Let's go show everyone the pictures of my son." I say with

THIRD TIME'S A CHARM

so much happiness and pride. I'm going to be the most amazing mother to this little boy. Even without Maysen.

****

"Guys I really appreciate you taking the time to show me the house. Are you sure you don't need it anymore Austin?"

"Nah, Leah's house she got from her grandparents is so big it makes much more sense that we live there and raise a family."

"I didn't pull you guys away from anything did I?"

"No. We were all sitting around the women's clinic waiting for our sister to have an ultrasound. It was no bother having to leave. Believe us."

"She got to see her baby for the first time I take it by all of you being present?"

"Yes. Like we told you before the loser father isn't in the picture so we're all trying to make up for his absence any way that she'll let us."

"That really is too bad that he isn't around. Does he know about the baby?"

"We don't really know too many details but I would imagine he does. Our sister isn't the type to just sleep around."

"I see. Well I wish her the best. Now, let's look at this house."

****

"Hey ladies. Wanna see a picture of your nephew??" I say with so much excitement. I plop down in the booth across from them and start to show them the pictures.

"OH MY GOODNESS! He looks so little Audrey!" Karlie screams and grabs my hands in both of hers.

113

"Doesn't he though? I can't believe I'm going to have a son!"

"You will be the best mother ever Audrey!"

"And you two will be the best aunts ever to this little boy!"

"Where's your Mom?" Leah says as the girls realize that I was there alone.

"She had to go meet with Ella Mae for something so I told her to go."

"Was she excited to hear it's a boy?" Leah asks.

"She cried and screamed. Did she do that when you had your ultrasounds?" I ask Karlie.

"Yes, every time. She and my mother were carrying on worse than Aiden and I were. It was so cute."

"I'm glad you had Aiden while you were going through this. I could only have ever wished for that kind of love and devotion. Maybe someday."

"Let's not go there. How about we go shopping for baby stuff?" Karlie asks, always the shopper of the three.

"I have to get back to the nursery but don't not go on my account. Next time."

"Ok, thank you for coming today. Tell Austin the good news for me will you?"

"Yes, I'll go find him right now. Love you three and congrats. Oh! I love you four!" Leah smiles and heads out of the café.

****

"Hey Princess, we're at my house. Showing it to the guy

from the garage. Ok see ya in a few." Austin hangs up his phone with a huge smile on his face.

"Aiden, Leah's walking over here. She's got some news to tell us. Must be about the ultrasound."

"Hope everything is okay." I say and pull myself away from the close family moment I feel as if I'm intruding on.

"No need to rush off. She's just around the corner. They all met for a cold one at the café after." Aiden says and looks mischievous.

"A cold one? I thought when a woman was pregnant she couldn't have alcohol?" I say with much more concern than I should have.

"Relax Man, I was joking. They only went for iced teas." We all chuckle at my misreading of that situation. Way to go moron.

"Whew, I was a little worried there. I've never been around anyone pregnant but I thought I had heard that and thought you're all hard core here."

Just as we're walking out of the house we see a red head walking up the driveway. Austin whistles big and takes off jogging down towards her. Must be his fiancé. They kiss and walk back up towards Aiden and I.

"Hey Princess, this is Maysen. He's taking over Sam's Garage. He's also going to rent my house so that I can move into your house completely. Maysen, this is my fiancée Leah."

I look at her and my breath catches because she's so beautiful. Just as beautiful as she was plastered all over the billboards and magazines.

"Nice to meet you Leah. You sure you don't want to keep this place to banish Austin to if he makes you mad?" I smile and shake her hand.

"No, I think there's a dog house out back at my house." She smiles back. "Nice to meet you though."

"So, what news did you want to tell us?" Aiden asks.

"You had better go find your wife and sister in a shop somewhere on Main St. and find out yourself."

"Done. See you all later." And he walks back the way that Leah had come.

"Your sister is going to have a little boy." Leah says to Austin making me feel like the intruder again.

"A nephew and a niece. How awesome. We need to set a date and have our own. You do know that don't you?"

"Yes Austin, we can set a date for today if you want."

"Hot damn, I'm getting married today!" He picks his fiancé up with ease and swings her around.

"You idiot we aren't really doing it today. Your mother, sister and sister in law would kill us if we didn't let them plan it."

"True. So, Maysen you want the house?"

"I think I do thank you. Just the right size for me and my Mom."

"You live with your Mom?" Leah asks with an inquisitive look on her face.

"She will live with me is more like it. She's in pretty bad health. Just got out of the hospital in Tulsa recently. She's the reason I moved back to Tulsa and then here."

"Where did you live before?"

"Leah, that's a lot of questions, playing detective or what?"

"It's okay, I'm an open book. I want people around here to trust me so I'll let you know anything you want to know."

"I'm sorry you don't have to answer any of my dumb questions." Leah says looking embarrassed for the inquisition.

"It's okay. I used to live in Omaha, Nebraska then moved back to Tulsa when my Mom was ready to be released from the hospital. She had pneumonia and was very ill for about six months."

"You used to live in Omaha. And you're a mechanic. And your Mom was ill in the hospital in Tulsa?" Leah asks as if she's fitting imaginary puzzle pieces together.

"Yes. I think that's what he said. We need to go Leah. You're going to scare the new mechanic away and I won't get my house rented. Sorry for Detective Leah here. Here are the keys to the house. It's yours."

"You're a good man, thank you. Take care. Goodbye Detective." I smile and walk past the couple whispering to each other. What a strange woman.

****

"Hey baby sister. I hear you have some news for me?" Aiden says as he finds us in a small shop on Main St.

"Yes, you're going to have a nephew."

"Wow that's great news! One of both! Congrats Aud!" He wraps me up in a big Aiden bear hug. I squeal with excitement and enjoy the warmth of his strong arms. The love for my family has filled me so full today and I pray it never stops. They are going to be so good to my son. To my son. To my son. That sounds so amazing to say.

"Where's Austin? Thought you two were together?" Karlie asks Aiden while handing his daughter to him.

"He's back at his house with Leah and the guy from the garage. He's gonna rent it to him."

"He and Leah need to set a date now. Nothing keeping them from it now."

"For sure. I bet they're talking about it now." Aiden leans down and sits Aleah in the stroller. "You're going to have a boy cousin Baby Doll."

"Audrey, can I take your maternity photos? I'm itching to do it. I've wanted to get back into the studio more now that Aleah's getting older."

"Of course. You set the appointment and I'll be there. Now I need to get back to class. The kids are eager to find out the gender too. Love you guys." I kiss each one on the cheek and head to my car.

I turn the ignition and nothing. The battery is dead. This can't be happening on this happy day. Oh well, I grab my stuff and walk to Karlie's car. They look a little surprised to see me coming back.

"My car's dead. Must be the battery." I tell Aiden.

"I'll take care of it. Karlie, can you take Audrey to work and come back to get me?"

"Yep. Let's go Aud. See you in a bit babe."

"What are you going to do with my car?"

"Get it fixed, duh."

"Whatever, thanks brother."

✱✱✱✱✱✱✱✱✱✱✱✱

"Hey Maysen, it's Aiden. I was hoping you could help. My little sister's car is dead in front of Sally's. Can you come look at it?"

"Sounds like a battery. I'll bring a spare and be right there."

"Thanks."

I grab an old battery off the floor and head to Sally's to help Aiden. I really like the guy and enjoy our friendship so of course I drop everything and go.

After replacing the battery in the car, I find that it's not just the battery. "I think it's the alternator too. I'll tow you to the shop. Is that okay? Do you need to talk to your sister first?"

"Nope. Let's get it taken care of. She's six months pregnant remember? She needs a reliable vehicle."

"Okay, here's the tow rope. Good thing it's only two blocks."

16

"Ma'am I was calling to let you know your car is done and ready to be picked up." I hear on the other end of the phone. I don't normally answer calls during school but since it's late afternoon and my car's in the shop, I did today.

"Thank you so much. I'll be there in a few minutes." That voice made my heart jump and goose bumps to appear on my arms. Why does that voice sound so familiar? It can't. You're just hormonal again and that's probably just heartburn. Once again I'm hearing things that aren't there and seeing people I'm not really seeing. Hearing one voice and seeing one man. Wonderful, I'm losing my mind now too.

"Mrs. Marlin, could you take over for a while? My car's in the shop and I was just told it's finished. I'll be only a little while." I rush off to get my car feeling as if I need the fresh air. Need something but I don't know what that is.

My phone is ringing and I see it's Leah so I answer.

"Hey Leah. How are you?"

"How are you? What are you doing? I figured I would get your voicemail."

"I'm walking to the garage to get my car. It's done. What're you doing?"

"Sitting here with Karlie and we were wondering what you were doing Saturday? We were thinking of going to Tulsa to do some baby shopping. Sound like something you want to do?"

"Very much so, yes. Thank you I look forward to it."

"Ok take care." Leah says and hangs up the phone. I put mine back in my purse and as I'm about to turn the corner onto the street the garage is on I see Austin standing by his pickup in front of the Drug Store.

"Hey stranger, what are you doing?" I ask as I hug him and smile.

"Waiting for you. Leah said you were walking to get your car? Aiden and I just delivered it to the school for you."

"Oh my goodness I didn't know that. The gentleman from the garage called to tell me it was done but not that you were delivering it."

"He didn't know either. We got there right after he called you. I'm sorry you walked this far. I'll take you back now."

"Ok thank you." I can't believe I walked this far when my car was in the parking lot at the school. Why didn't I even look for it first? Duh, I didn't know it was there.

****

"Hey Maysen, is our sister's car done?" Austin says from the doorway of the garage.

"Yes, just called her and told her. She's on her way to get

it."

"We'll deliver it to her. Thanks for fixing it though. I should have had you do an oil change while you had it in here. When's your next appointment opening?"

"I'm thinking next Friday at three. Does that work for your sister?"

"It will. I'll bring it in around lunchtime. Thanks again. Send us the bill." They walk out and one hops into the newly fixed car and one the pickup. Such good brothers.

I start to write down the name for the appointment but realize that I don't even know their sister's name. I shake it off and just write Blake. That'll have to work.

****

"Karlie, she's on for going Saturday. I'm telling you this guy is her guy. He used to live in Omaha, worked at a garage, his mother was in the hospital with pneumonia in Tulsa, and he's recently moved. His name is even Maysen. I didn't ask for his last because I already sounded stupid asking all the questions I did ask. He and Austin were calling me detective."

"Leah there's no way this is the same guy. That would be the biggest act of fate if it was. No way. Just a lot of coincidences."

"He is hot and looks just like what she described."

"I saw him the other day when I picked up Mom's car. I didn't think anything of him being Audrey's baby daddy. There's just no way Leah."

"We have got to get them together. Have to. If it's not him then it's no harm done right?"

"I guess not but how in the world are you going to do that without the guys realizing what you're doing? If by some humongous chance he is Prince Charming, Aiden and Austin are going to kill him. You do realize that right?"

"Oh I hadn't thought about those two. We just can't let them figure out who he is."

"IF he is who you think he is Leah."

"I know it's a long shot but it's all so perfect. It has to be him Karlie. Has to be."

"Oh boy what did you have in mind?"

"This weekend when we are ready to leave town for Tulsa, we need to have the guys invite him out to the ranch for a barbeque and when we get home he'll be there. And kaboom when they see each other again it will be fireworks!"

"And her brothers will string him up right then!"

"Then it's up to us to keep a handle on our men. Audrey loves this guy so much and she needs him. Whether we want to admit it or not, this baby boy needs his daddy too."

"I know. Fine, tell me what I need to do. Please don't make me regret this. I'm going to regret this aren't I?"

17

"Hey Aiden, I'm sorry I can't make it tonight. My Mom's not feeling very well. I'm going to stick around the house. Thanks again for the invite. Have a good night." I hang up my phone a little disappointed I couldn't make the Blake barbeque but Mom's health is more important.

"Feeling better Ma? You need to rest but if you want some soup I can get it."

"No, you go to that barbeque and have fun with your new friends."

"I'm staying right here with you. Aunt Ingrid isn't here to take care of you so I'm doing it. I really don't mind. You're the most important person to me so I'm staying put tonight. There will be more than enough time for other barbeques."

"You're a wonderful son. Do you think I'll ever see you as a father? I know you would be a wonderful one. And a wonderful husband."

"Ma, that's not even close to happening. Let's get you some soup."

"Maysen Michael Correli, you need to go find that girl. You're so hung up on her you can't think straight."

"Mom we've been over this before. She's gone. I don't know where she is."

"What was her name at least? You did get that didn't you?"

"Audrey. That's all I'm saying and I'm going to go make your soup."

****

"Karlie that was Austin. He called to tell me that the barbeque has been cancelled because the man of honor couldn't make it. His mom's ill tonight. Dangit so it isn't going to happen tonight."

"Oh well. If this is the guy she's talked about they're bound to run into each other. This is a very small town you know. I'm surprised they haven't already."

"I know. I was so mad at Austin for delivering her car the other day. She was on her way to the garage to get it when they swooped in and had to be heroes."

"What are you two whispering about over here? I was paying for all this baby stuff you helped me pick out and you're over here whispering like school girls. What gives?"

"Nothing, just talking about the barbeque getting cancelled."

"Oh well I wasn't up for that anyway. This trip to Tulsa seems longer now that I have to pee every ten minutes."

"Ha! Told you that was going to happen!" Karlie yells and smiles that big Karlie smile.

"Are you ready to go home? We have that long drive again.

Let's see if we can get farther before either of you have to stop to pee along-side the road this time."

18

"Aiden, what are you doing here?" I ask as I see my brother in the door way to my classroom. He never comes here. "Is everything okay?"

"It's fine. Don't panic I'm just here to get your car. When we picked it up last week, we made another appointment for today to get the oil changed. We can't have you driving a car that's not reliable."

"My car is two years old Aiden. I think it's fine."

"Yes, but now that you're going to have a child with you; we need to take extra good care of it. Maintenance is even more important now."

"Whatever you say. You're not going to listen to me anyway."

"You're so smart. No wonder you're the teacher in the family."

"Thank you. I'll get a ride to the garage after my tutoring session. It'll be around 5:30. Will that be enough time?"

"That should be perfect. See you soon. Love you."

"Thanks Aiden. Tell Austin thanks too. You guys might be overbearing but I love you."

He walks away with my keys leaving me stranded once again at the school. How long is this going to go on? They are being very attentive. Probably until this baby boy graduates college.

****

"Hey guys, you got the car again? Is she going to come get it tonight or do I need to deliver it to her?"

"She's going to get a ride from school once her tutoring session is over. She thinks it'll be around 5:30. Is that too late?"

"No, that's perfect. I'm usually wrapping things up around then anyway. Thanks guys. Appreciate the work."

"No problem. Just take good care of our sister's car. She has our nephew to take care of now too. And since she'll be a single mom she needs us to help out where we can."

"She's lucky to have you two."

****

"Hey Princess, what's up? Aiden and I just dropped Audrey's car off at the garage, why? Yes, we're leaving it. Yes, I'll be back at the nursery in a few. Yes, he's going home why? What are you up to? Okay be right there."

"The women are up to something. Karlie has been over curious about Maysen. And Leah went off with twenty questions too the other day."

"Leah just asked me if you were going home and if I was coming to the nursery right now. I get the feeling she doesn't want us picking up Audrey's car this time."

128

"Maybe Audrey told them we were hovering too much. I'm sure that's what it is. She always has hated us boys trying to protect her."

"Probably. I guess she can pick up her own car tonight then. Oh well, see you late brother."

****

"Hey Kim! Could I get a ride to Sam's Garage? My car should be done by now."

"Of course. Are you ready now? Let's go. I'll drop you off on my way to meet my mother at Sally's."

"Thank you so much. My brothers seemed to think my car needed some maintenance done on it." I say rolling my eyes.

"They're just taking care of their little sister and nephew."

"I know but it's more like smothering. I can't even make my own appointments for my car. I have a feeling it's never going to change now with this baby coming."

"Probably not. Karlie had an issue with Aiden a time or two didn't she?"

"Still does!" I say laughing.

When we pull up to the garage and I thank Kim for the ride, I grab my stuff from the back seat and walk to my car. I lay my bag and jacket in the front seat only taking my wallet with me. If my brothers haven't already paid, I'll need it but I'm sure that's taken care of too.

I walk in the front door and hear the little bell over it jingle. I don't see anyone in the front office so I start through the door to the back area.

Before I get three steps in I see a man with his back to me

and I'm struck with shock and frozen in place. Oh my goodness this can't be. This has to be another one of my hallucinations. This can't be the one man I haven't gotten out of my head.

The unknown man turns around and once his eyes lock with mine he is also stunned. He too is unable to speak or believe he's seeing who he's seeing either. How can this truly be him?

"Um, I'm here to get my car. It's the white one outside. Um, is it ready?" Is all I can spit out. Amazed that I could speak even that much I self-consciously try to cover my stomach. He can't find out about the baby this way. He can't seem to find any words and can't quit looking at my face then down at my stomach then back to my face.

"Y-y-y-yes. It's finished."

"What do I owe you?"

"Aiden already paid for it. You're their little sister? Audrey Blake. Oh my goodness I should have put two and two together."

"What are you doing here? How did you get here? Why are you here?"

"My uncle owns it. Sam's my uncle."

"Wow. Just wow. This world is so small I don't believe it."

"I didn't think I would ever see you again. After, well never mind about that. You look beautiful as ever."

"Thank you. I didn't think I would ever see you again either."

"You live here in Colvin?"

"Yes. All my life."

"Wow all along you were right here. Incredible."

"I can't believe you're really here in front of me again. I honestly never expected to set eyes on you again."

"I'm sorry to disappoint you then."

"No, I didn't mean that. I just didn't think I would run into you a third time."

"Seems fate has it in for us for some reason."

"I would say so. Well, I really need to get going. It was so nice to see you again."

"You too Audrey. Take care of yourself. If your car breaks down again, you know who to call."

"Yes, thank you. Take care. Bye Maysen."

And with that I walked out of that garage as fast I can possibly go. How in the world in all the mechanic shops in the entire world do I run into my dream man in this one? How in the world did I not know he was here? He's the one everyone has been going on and on about for weeks! All the while it was Maysen. My Maysen.

I whip out of the parking lot as quick as I safely could but once I'm around the corner out of sight I stop my car and pull to the side of the road. Emotions are boiling over now and I can't seem to keep the tears at bay any longer.

The tears flow like a river and I cry like it's the last thing I can do on Earth. How in the world do I deal with this now? I am in such shock from seeing the man I'm so madly in love with standing in front of me in my hometown. I just can't believe this. How can this be true?

He's been all chummy with my brothers and father too. Oh my goodness. My brothers. When they find out Maysen is my baby's father they are going to murder him. Oh my goodness that adds even more dimension to this craziness.

After bawling my eyes out and running my tear ducts dry, I pull myself together and head home. I have got to figure this all out and soon before Maysen realizes that this is his baby and before my brothers figure out the same thing.

****

Oh my goodness I can't believe Audrey lives here in Colvin. And she was just standing in front of me again. And her brothers have been in here for the past couple weeks. And she's pregnant. She looks so beautiful and glowing. Whomever the baby belongs to is lucky to have her as the mother of their child. Oh wait, the guys said the father wasn't around. He was some loser that knocked her up and never looked back.

STOP THE PRESS! Can this seriously be my baby? Holy crap! I just left her in the hotel room because I thought she was ashamed. What if she got pregnant that night? Holy crap! Holy crap! That was about the perfect time I think from what her brothers said. Holy crap!

What do I do now? Carter, I have to call Carter.

"Hey Man, what's up? How's the business?"

"Good. Good. Hey remember that girl I told you about? The one from the Tulsa hospital and then that one night in Omaha?"

"The one you can't forget? That girl?"

"Yes. Yes. She lives here in Colvin. She's Aiden's little sister. She just came to pick up her car."

"Are you freaking out? You've been there for a couple weeks and you just found this out? Didn't you like go get beers with her brothers? That's so wicked!"

"Dude it gets more wicked. She's like six months pregnant too."

"Whoa Dude! You think it's yours don't you?"

"They said it was some loser that knocked her up and left her. I left her in that hotel room."

"Yeah but you thought she was ashamed of your roll in the hay so you spared her the morning after talk."

"Yes but it's all too much of a coincidence. What the hell do I do now?"

"Dude I'm at a loss here. I don't have a clue."

"Holy crap. Holy crap."

"How did she look? The same as you've remembered?"

"The most beautiful woman I have ever seen Carter. And her little stomach sticking out there. Oh my goodness that could be my child in there."

"Whoa, you need to talk to her before you start seeing pink and blue."

"I know but what the hell do I say? Hey Audrey, I know you're a good girl and all but since you threw caution to the wind and slept with me, did you do that again after me and get pregnant?"

"Um probably not like that you moron."

"No kidding. I don't have a clue what to do here."

"Good luck. Keep me posted."

"Thanks a lot for the help. Not."

I hang up the phone with Carter and I'm even more convinced that that baby is mine. Audrey is carrying my baby. I just know it. My Audrey is carrying our baby. Our baby.

****

"Mom, I really need to talk to someone right now." I walk into her craft room where she's making a quilt for the baby.

"Sure honey, what's wrong? You look like you've been crying."

"I'm okay just completely confused."

"About what honey?"

"The baby's father. I saw him today and I don't know what to do about it."

"How did you see the baby's father? I thought he didn't live here? I think you need to rewind and tell me all of it from the beginning."

I settle in on the sofa and Mom joins me as I begin where I was watching Aleah through the hospital window and all the way up to present day. I should have done this months ago but I was so ashamed of what I had done and how I had run Maysen off that last morning. I should have known my Mom wouldn't judge.

****

"Mom, there's something I need to tell you before the news hits and you hear it from someone else."

"What's wrong Maysen? What happened?"

"Remember the girl you've been telling me to go find that stole my heart?"

"The one you told me you didn't know where she was and no way to ever see her again?"

"Yes. Well I saw her today. She lives here in Colvin of all places."

"Oh my goodness Maysen fate really does want you two together. No one gets three chances at a life with their true love. Who is she?"

"Audrey Blake."

"Maysen Michael Correli! How do you even know her?"

"I met her in the hospital in Tulsa you were in. Aiden's baby was born there."

"That's why she was there."

"Yes and now there's more Ma."

"Maysen what is it? You're trembling."

"She pregnant Ma and I'm almost convinced it's my baby."

"Oh my Heavens! I'm going to be a Grandma!!"

"Ma, we don't know that and you can't say anything. I don't even know where to go from here. We both were so shocked to see each other that small talk is all we could manage."

"Son, that's amazing. You get to see her again. This time you know where she is and exactly how to get ahold of her. I would hope that third time's a charm for you two."

"What do I do? I don't want to scare her but I'm also angry because I have had a child growing inside of her for months now and I didn't even know. I could possibly be a father this fall and I had no idea. Could be. I mean it's possible it could be someone else's but Audrey's not that type of girl."

"She isn't. I'm surprised she got that close to you."

"Thanks Ma. That makes me feel wonderful."

"I didn't mean it like that and you know it. She's always been a very good girl. That's all I meant."

"I know. We talked for hours the last night I saw her in Omaha. I'm not sure why she slept with me but she was so ashamed of it the next morning I left before she had to face me."

"Oh Maysen. You need to talk to her. And soon before you worry yourself sick over this baby."

"I'm not just worried about the baby. I'm worried about Audrey too. She's been doing this all along by herself."

"Well you're here now. She can rest easy now. Do you love her?"

"Very much I highly doubt she rests very easy for a while." Or me. I could very possibly have a child in a few months. I have to marry Audrey if that's my baby. Even if it's not, I want to marry Audrey. I want to spend the rest of my life with her. And our baby.

★★★★★★★★★★★★

"We need to get the rest of the family in here honey." Mom says after we're back to present with the Maysen and Audrey saga.

"Mom I don't want the boys to know yet. They'll murder Maysen and I just found him again. I know he's not going anywhere this time, but I just need time to figure this out before anyone else has to know."

"I have to tell your father though."

"I know. He won't murder him but won't that be a shock to know he's the baby's father. And Dad's known him since he's been here in Colvin." I shake my head.

"We have been wanting to set you up with him too because he's such a wonderful young man. And now we know he's the one in your heart already it's even better."

"Mom no matchmaking. I can do this myself."

"You've done such a wonderful job the past two times. I just pray third time's a charm for you two. There's going to be three of you in it soon. Better get a move on it my dear."

"I know. Thank you Mom for hearing me out. I love you." I get up and hug my mother. Without her I really don't know where I would be today.

"I love you more my dearest daughter. Go make things right and you'll feel right again too."

I only wish I felt so confident. Maysen could very well be mad at me for not letting him know months ago that he was going to be a father. And now he's here and I just ran away like a scared school girl. He was so ashamed of our night together and I'm not sure I can deal with that shame again when he finds out it created a life. He might think I'm trying to trap him.

I send a quick text to my sisters in law.

My house. 30 minutes. 911

Of course I get immediate responses saying they'll be right here. I walk back to my apartment above the garage and straight to what will be my son's room. I see Aiden and Austin got the walls painted the shade of pale blue that I picked out. They also started to assemble the furniture. Maysen will want to do that I'm sure. Will he really want to be here with me though? He'll want a nursery in his own house. This is even worse than not knowing where he was. I sit down in the glider rocker and hang my head in my hands.

"Sweet girl, what's wrong? You said it was an emergency." I hear Karlie say as she and Leah rush into my house twenty or so minutes later. Right on time.

"I found Maysen."

"Where? How?" Leah shrieks.

"He's the new mechanic at the garage in town."

"I knew it!! I told you Karlie. I told you that was him!"

"Leah? You knew he was here and you didn't tell me? How could you?"

"I only figured it out a while ago. We've been trying to get you two in the same place for over a week. Remember the barbeque? That's when it was going to first happen. Then we made sure the boys didn't get the car for you. We wanted you to find him on your own."

"Oh my goodness. Do my brothers know? They'll murder him."

"No. We haven't told them. That's up to you to do. In your own time." Karlie says and hugs me tightly.

"What are you going to do? How did the meeting go?" Leah asks while squeezing my hands.

I tell them all the details and they both sit there like children hearing their favorite bedtime story. How did they know about this and not tell me? How in the world did they figure it out?

"How did you figure this out?"

"Well, I saw him that day of the ultrasound at Austin's house and I kinda grilled the poor guy not realizing who he was. He told us about his mom being sick, moving from Omaha and Tulsa. You know everything started to add up. But of course I wasn't sure because I had never seen a picture of him."

"When Leah told me about it I didn't believe it. But then Aiden told me about his mom being in the Tulsa hospital about the same time that Aleah was born. And that he was hung up on some girl he met before coming here."

"You all were planning on setting him up weren't you?"

"Yes. With you. Your parents have wanted to since your

dad met him. We just didn't know his name was Maysen."

"Or that he was the one you've been crying over for six months." Leah says and hugs me again.

"Wow. Maybe third time's a charm? How do I talk to him about this? He was ashamed of what we did, remember? How's he going to feel about a baby coming from it?"

"You don't know for sure that that's what happened."

"Oh my goodness this is such a mess!" I scream and throw myself back in the glider. This is unbelievable actually. How do two people get thrown together three times in a lifetime when most people never have one chance? Heck I'm probably hormonal and this isn't quite as amazing as it seems.

"You need to get some sleep Audrey. You can deal with things tomorrow if you choose to. We love you and are only a phone call away."

"Thanks girls. Love you so much!" I hug both of them goodbye and lock the door. I make myself a cup of pregnancy tea and go upstairs to try to sleep. Today was very eventful and very emotional.

19

"Good morning class. Today we're going to cover division. Does anyone already know how to do division?" I ask my class a couple of days later. It's Friday and I'm looking very forward to holing myself up in my apartment and not coming out until Monday morning. No people, no phone, no internet, and definitely no thoughts of Maysen. Yeah right who am I kidding?

"Miss Blake? Miss Blake? Are you alright?" I hear from my doorway. It's Mrs. Simms. She's looking at me with concern on her face.

"Oh I'm sorry I was deep in thought. Zoned out. Very sorry. What can I do for you?"

"These came for you a few minutes ago. I thought you might like to display them on your desk." She holds up the most amazing vase of flowers I have ever seen. Looks like every flower the shop could have in it.

"But who are they from? My brothers are going to pay if they're from them." I say looking for the card. No card. That's weird I figure they would want me to know. Then a slight thought slips into my mind. Maysen. Surely he didn't send them. He wouldn't send me flowers. Right?

"Have a good rest of your day Miss Blake."

"Thank you for bringing them to me and have a good day yourself." I say as she walks away back down the hallway to the front office.

I take out my phone to text the girls. They'll know who sent them.

Got flowers. Who?

I hit send and wait for their replies. They'll tell me they're from themselves probably.

Not us. Prince Charming?

Of course they wouldn't admit to it. I should have known. Oh well I'll deal with them later. For now I'll enjoy the beautiful arrangement and let it brighten my day a little more.

Later as I'm walking out the front doors of the school to head home, I hear Mrs. Marlin holler my name from the office.

"Audrey, the card for your flowers fell off and was on the floor. Thought you might want to know who those beautiful things came from. Have a great weekend."

"Thank you. You too. See you Monday." I walk to my car but feel afraid to open the card now. Why? Just open it and find out it's from the family. Who else would they be from?

So great to see you again. Maysen

Oh my goodness! They are from him! Why would he do something so sweet? He didn't want me in Omaha so why be so nice now? This is so confusing!

I'll just drive right over there and give him a piece of my mind. And that's exactly what I intend on doing until I pull up in front of the shop and see him bent over a vehicle with no shirt on.

Oh my goodness. What was I coming here for again? Oh my.

****

"Audrey? What are you doing sitting in your car in front of the shop? Is it not running right?" I see her sitting there when I turn to go back inside to get another wrench.

"Um um n-n-no I was um I'm not really sure what I'm doing. I'm sorry I need to go. You look hot. I mean busy."

What is going on with her? She can't make complete sentences and she's shaking. I look down into my hands an see my shirt, maybe I should put it on. Her reaction to my bare chest makes me smile.

I decide for some stupid reason to walk around to her passenger side and get in. Once I'm sitting next to her in the car I turn and look at her. Oh my I've forgotten just how beautiful she is. My dreams and thoughts haven't done her justice.

"Audrey, what's going on with you? I see you got my flowers. Did you like them?"

"Of course I did they're very pretty. Why did you send them though?"

"I wanted you to know that I was happy to have seen you the other day. Did I upset you by sending them? I'm sorry if I did."

"No, they were a beautiful surprise. I've never gotten flowers before. Thank you very much. I just don't understand why is all. I guess I came here to ask that."

"Audrey, I have thought about you every day since the last time I saw you in Omaha."

"But you left me Maysen. You didn't want to face what we had done."

"Oh my goodness Audrey is that what you've thought all this time? I thought you felt that way when you snuck into the bathroom. That was the most amazing night of my life. I haven't stopped reliving it since."

"Maysen I only went into the bathroom because I had never woken up next to a man before and wanted to make sure I didn't look horrible or have smelly breath for when you woke up. I was coming back to bed as soon as I was done. But you were gone by then. Never to be seen again."

"Until the other day. You really do look beautiful Audrey. I haven't forgotten you or stopped thinking about you."

"Oh Maysen I just don't know anything anymore."

"Is the baby's father going to be around at all?"

"I hope so but I'm not sure how he'll feel when he finds out."

"I see. Well, I hope he does come around for your sake and the baby's."

"Thank you for the flowers Maysen they were truly a brightness in my day."

"You're welcome. You take care of yourself Audrey. Good luck. You'll make a wonderful mother. That's a lucky kid to have you and your family around it."

And with that I walk away. Walk away from the one woman I now know I can't have. If there's a possibility that the baby's father could come around, she needs to have him. Not me. I would only complicate things even more. I wish her all the best but now my heart's broken even more.

****

"Oh my goodness Audrey why didn't you just tell him right

then that he's the baby's father? The poor guy was trying to pour his heart out to you." Leah says to me while the three of us are sitting on my patio later that evening.

"I panicked. I was afraid he wouldn't want me and wasn't sure what I had heard him say. He really did say he has been thinking about me ever since right? Or am I making this up?"

"Honey you're the only one that knows for sure what was said. But if you're telling us word for word then yes that's what he's saying."

"Karlie are you sure? Leah?"

"I think you made another big mistake with him. You need to talk to him and that was your shot. You blew it big time."

"Aaaahhhh! Why is this so damned hard?"

"It's life sweetie." Mom says as she walks in on the conversation.

"Hey Mom. How are you?"

"How are you girls doing? Especially you Miss Heart Breaker."

"You heard all that did you?"

"Yes Audrey I heard it all as I was walking up here. You weren't exactly quiet about it."

"No one else is with you are they?" I panic.

"You mean your brothers? No they aren't. I believe they're in town with Prince Charming as you two call him. I think they're helping him get moved in." Mom smiles at Leah and Karlie.

"Have you seen him? He's very dreamy." Karlie says and laughs. "But of course not as hunky as my husband."

"Nice save. I have heard he's handsome yes. There are a lot of whispers around town about him. I think some of the ladies from church were going to try to set him up with their daughters and nieces."

"No. They can't do that. He can't date anyone in town."

"Audrey then you need to go talk to him."

"Fine. I'll go right now." I can't believe I'm going to town again. Going to talk to Maysen. Maysen of all people. Never thought I would say that again. I'm going to go talk to Maysen in person. A part of me dreads it but then there's the traitorous side who is excited.

****

After having the guys help move some boxes into the new house, I say to Mom, "I'm not sure what there is to make for dinner tonight. How about we go to Sally's."

"That sounds nice. I'll go freshen up and then we can go."

Uncle Sam and Aunt Ingrid extended their vacation another two weeks so Mom and I will have a little time to get moved into Austin's house. Oh good grief I wonder if Aiden, AJ and Austin know I slept with Audrey? They'll probably kill me if they find out. They'll pull all their work from the shop and I'll lose my chance of buying it.

"I'm ready son. Let's go. You can be my date tonight."

"Works for me." I walk Mom to the car but I secretly wish it were Audrey and I that are on an actual date. Once again my mind flashes back to our dinner date in Omaha. My heart feels like it breaks into another sliver as I realize that some other man will get to love her for the rest of her life.

"Where do you want to sit Ma? The window booth over here is open."

"That's a good one. That's a pretty girl sitting over there Maysen. Do you see her?"

"Yes Ma I see her. Let's order, I'm starving."

"Don't you want to meet a pretty young lady and have a family?"

"Mom, where is this all coming from? I told you the other day about Audrey."

"Audrey? What about her? Have you met her? She's such a pretty girl too. Are you interested in her?"

"What? Mom are you feeling okay?" I'm starting to get very concerned. She doesn't even remember our talk about Audrey. She never forgets talks about Grandkids and my getting hitched.

"I'm just fine son. When you graduate from college we'll find you a wife so I can have some Grandkids. Doesn't that sound nice?"

Graduate from college? What? Whoa, what is going on here?

"Ma, I'm not in college anymore. It's 2014. You know that right?"

"Sure. Sure. Let's eat. I haven't been to Sally's since before I moved to Tulsa. You used to love eating here too Michael."

"Michael? Ma why did you just call me by Dad's name? Are you sure you're doing okay?"

"Of course I know who you are. We're getting married soon aren't we?"

"Let's go Ma. We need to go." I have got to get her out of here and to a hospital. This is the strangest thing I have ever heard. She thinks I'm my Dad and they're getting married soon. This is so bizarre and terrifies me.

As we rush outside of Sally's and towards the car I hear a female voice calling my name from down the sidewalk.

"Maysen! Maysen!" I turn to see Audrey coming towards us. Even in the terrified state that I'm in I can't help but be relieved to see her.

"Audrey, I can't talk right now. Something's wrong with my Mom. She's talking very strange and thinks I'm my Dad."

"Didn't your Dad leave before you were born?" She asks also starting to become alarmed.

"Yes. I don't understand what's happening."

"Hello dear. So glad to see you again. When are you two going to set a date? Looks like you need to set one before that baby comes."

"Wow, this is weird. Let me help you get her to the after-hours clinic." Audrey takes Mom by the hand and helps her into the backseat of my car. What she does next shocks me even more. She gets into the front seat and waits for me to back out.

"You're going with us? Don't you have somewhere to be?"

"Not right now no. I want to help you and your Mom. Hurry."

I do just that. I hurry Mom to the clinic. Audrey calls ahead and has them waiting with a wheelchair when we arrive. Of course Mom puts up such a big fuss and they let her walk in by herself.

****

"Thank you for being here." I hear Maysen say to me. I thought he was sleeping but that must have been me that was.

"It's no big deal. I pray she's okay. Shouldn't they know

147

anything yet?"

"You would think. I really do appreciate the help and the company. I'll be okay if you need to go. Really."

"No, I'm good where I am. You need a friend right now. I'm here. Can I be that friend for you? At least for right now?"

"Of course." That's all he says and leans back in his chair again. It's been a little over an hour since we brought his mother in here and no word yet on her condition.

"My brothers are on their way."

"How are we going to explain how we know each other?"

"For right now we'll say I saw you outside Sally's and helped out."

"You want to lie?"

"For now it's fine. The whole truth can wait." The entire whole truth can wait.

****

"Mr. Correli? Are you Maysen Correli?" I'm awoken by the sound of a nurse standing in front of me. I open my eyes and see an older lady with scrubs touching my knee trying to wake me. I look to the side expecting to see an empty chair but to my surprise Audrey is still here. And her brothers are all across from us stretched out in chairs asleep also. In the midst of something so terrifying with my mother, they are such amazing friends that they wanted to stay and support me.

"Yes I'm Maysen. How's my Mother?" I stand up hoping the lady will take me to see my Mom.

"She's resting comfortably and the doctor would like to see you in her room." She looks around at the people there with me.

"Just you though. Only immediate family is allowed right now."

"That's fine I'll be right there." I walk over to Audrey and put my hand on her shoulder to wake her. She startles awake and I do the same with Aiden and Austin.

"Wow I didn't realize we were sleeping here. We really can sleep anywhere can't we?" Aiden chuckles and stretches.

"They called me in to see my Mom. You guys go home and get some rest. I really appreciate your support. Audrey, you especially need a bed to sleep in." I see her frown at me but stand up and stretch.

"You sure you want me to go? I'm okay here if you need me." She says and I know deep down she really does mean it. You can always tell when someone is being insincere but Audrey is the polar opposite of insincere. I want so badly to tell her yes I need her to stay with me.

"I'm fine. They won't let anyone else in anyway. You might as well go home and get a comfortable nap." I squeeze her shoulder and smile. When she smiles back at me it knocks my socks off, I sigh a big relief that I have her in my life again. Even if it's just in the friend capacity. I wave goodbye and follow the nurse to my mother's room.

"Your mother is waking up but still seems a bit disoriented. She was severely dehydrated and that was allowing her mind to drift to other places and times. We don't see any signs of illness or causes of concern. We'll keep her for a little longer for observation but she should make a full recovery. She was very lucky that you were with her and brought her in so quickly."

"Thank you. So she hasn't been drinking enough fluids? That can cause her to think I'm my father thirty years ago?"

"I'm very sorry this happened to her but she does need to drink more fluids and keep hydrated. We'll get her back to perfect health and then you can bring her home again."

"Okay thank you Doctor. Ma? Can you hear me? It's Maysen."

"Hi honey. How're you doing? Why am I in the hospital? Is this a hospital?"

"You had an episode Mom because you haven't been getting enough fluids. I had to bring you here so they could help. They want to keep you a while just to be on the safe side."

"Maysen you have a new business to run and you-know-who to win over. You need to focus more on that than your old Mom here."

"No chance of that. I'm worried about you and everything else can wait. I haven't taken very good care of you since we got here and that's about to change."

"You're so hard headed. Just promise me you won't give up on her and that baby."

"Ma she helped me bring you here and she stayed here with me all night until they let me come back here. I think things are good with us so don't worry about that. You need to get better and take care of yourself."

"Maysen I will be fine. I think I've just gotten lazy since Ingrid left. You know she kept me going and I think I got used to that. I'll do better I promise. Go live your life son."

"Not arguing with you now. You need to rest. I need to get the shop opened up. I have a few people this morning but I can come back after lunch to check on you. If you need me just call."

"Maysen I'll be fine, just go."

"Okay. I love you Ma." I kiss her on the forehead and head out the door. I really thought I was going to lose her last night. That was so strange. I am so thankful for Audrey being there with me while I was waiting on the doctor. She was so tender to Mom when we were trying to get her out of the car and into the wheelchair. I should have known Mom wouldn't go in it and she calls me hard headed?

20

"Maysen? It's Audrey. I was calling to check on your Mom but I wasn't sure if you would be at the shop today or not." I say once he answers the phone.

"I just got here actually. She ran me off and made me come get some work done. She's going to be fine."

"I'm so glad she's going to be okay. That was scary."

"It was. They said as long as she stays hydrated she'll be just fine. They want to keep her for a while for observation though."

"That's probably best. That way in case it happens again they can be there to help."

"I wonder if she needs transferred to Tulsa's hospital? The clinic has only those couple of rooms. Do you think the doctor here is good enough?"

"Maysen, she'll be fine. The doctor here is great. Don't worry so much."

THIRD TIME'S A CHARM

"It's my Mom though. I can't help but worry."

"I know and you're a great son. You need to let the doctors help her though. You're a mechanic not a doctor."

"Point taken. I really need to get busy so I can go by there after lunch. Thanks again for helping me last night and staying."

"It was no big deal. Anything for a friend." One step at a time.

"Bye Audrey." I hear him say but know there was much more he wanted to say about the friend part of my answer.

I'm not sure I can be just friends with Maysen though. Not when all I want to do is jump into his arms and kiss him like there's no tomorrow. He looked so pained last night while waiting for the doctor. My heart just broke watching him pace the floor. I am so glad she's going to be okay. When Karlie lost her dad it was one of the toughest days for her and I don't wish that on anyone. Especially Maysen.

After hanging up with Maysen I leave the school and drive over to Stampley's to see Leah. She can help me work through this better than anyone.

"Hey you! What's up? How's Maysen's Mom?"

"He says she's going to be fine. She was just dehydrated. They're going to keep her for a bit to make sure she's okay."

"That's a relief. I bet Maysen is relieved too."

"He is. The whole time we were worried that something was wrong with his mom I couldn't help but feel guilty that if she passed away she would never know she had a grandson on the way. I have got to tell him. But how do I do that?"

"I wondered about that. I knew you would be struggling with your own demons the whole time. Austin said you never left

Maysen's side though. The guys think something's going on between you two now."

"Great. That's all I need is for my over protective brothers butting in."

"I told Austin to stay out of it but who knows if he'll listen to me."

"Wonderful. I'll see you later. I have to get back to class."

"You need to tell the poor guy."

I just frown and glare at her before turning and leaving the nursery. It's so easy for them to say. Just tell him Audrey. Yes, it's that easy. I guess Leah knows how hard something is to tell the one you love when you're afraid it will drive them away. She told Austin though and he loves her more today than before. Maybe Maysen will be the same way. It's now or never I guess.

Pulling up in front of the garage, I find myself overwhelmed with nerves and nausea. What am I doing here again? I can't think this is the time to tell him can I? I'm here and it's killing me knowing he doesn't have a clue about his son. I get out of the car and take a deep breath and exhale. Okay, let's get this over with.

"Hey Audrey, what brings you by? I just told you I was okay. Really, I am."

"I know you are but we need to talk Maysen."

"Okay about what? I thought we got it all out there and decided to be friends. Or at least try to be? Have you changed your mind?"

"There's more I need to tell you."

"More? Like what? It's okay you can tell me. After thinking I was going to lose my Mom again last night I decided to live day to day. What happened between us can stay in that hotel room, it doesn't need to haunt us here."

"Actually it can't stay in that hotel room Maysen."

"I don't understand."

"Maysen the father of my baby isn't some loser out there. My baby's father is standing right in front of me." I look straight into his eyes and see the confusion.

"What? You mean you're carrying my baby? Audrey?"

"Yes Maysen. There has never been anyone else. No one but you."

"Whoa. I need to sit down. You're telling me for six months you've known you were carrying my baby? Why didn't you tell me?"

"For one, I didn't have a way to contact you. The girls and I went to Omaha a while back to find you but some really nasty guy at that Ned's said you had moved and he didn't know where. I had no idea how to find you."

"You came to Omaha to find me? Audrey I'm so sorry you did that. That must have been hard on you. But when you saw me the other day you didn't tell me either."

"I know and I'm sorry about that. I was so shocked to see you that I didn't know what to do. I was afraid you would be angry with me or think I'm trying to trap you with the baby."

"Why would you think that?"

"The way you ran out of the hotel room. I honestly thought all along that you were ashamed of sleeping with me. I was afraid you wouldn't want to be around the baby. Or me."

"Oh my goodness Audrey that's so far from the truth. I have wanted you since the moment I laid eyes on you in the Tulsa hospital. I have kicked myself in the butt every day for not getting a way to keep in touch with you. And now we're going to have a baby?" He walks forward until he's within arm's length and motions towards my stomach as if asking for permission to touch it.

"Of course you can touch your son." I see his eyes light up and fill with tears.

"A son? You're having a boy? Oh my goodness Audrey! I can't believe I'm going to be a father. I had my suspicions but never dreamed it would be true. A son. Wow." He lightly touches my stomach and miraculously the baby moves at that moment as if high fiving his father. Maysen's eyes get as big as half dollars and he smiles bigger than I've ever seen.

"I felt that! My son is in there. Audrey, I love you. I love our son too." I let out a big gasp as he puts his hands on either side of my face and kisses me. Kisses me so gently and sweeter than I have ever felt before. My heart jumps and I feel as if I'm going to faint. I'm so happy and love this man so much I never expected this fairy tale to come true. I wrap my arms around his neck and pull him as close as I can.

"Maysen I love you so much too. I've been so miserable without you. I thought I would never be able to give my son his father. When I saw you the other day I was beyond happy. Would you like to see pictures of him?" I pull away from his arms and reach into my purse for the sonogram pictures.

"Of course I do." He takes them from my hands and holds them so lightly you would think they were fragile. The look on his face was so full of wonderment that I start to cry.

"Audrey? Why are you crying?" He wraps me up in his arms again.

"I just can't believe this is all happening. When I left Omaha I whole heartedly thought we would never get another chance of seeing each other. I thought my son was going to grow up with just a mother."

"Never. I will be there for him forever. And you. I will always be here for you too."

"Do you promise me? You're not mad at me?"

"How can I be mad? You went to Omaha that tells me you had every intention of telling me about the baby. I'm sorry you went all that way to leave so broken hearted. I will never ever let you feel that bad again as long as I live. Do you hear me Audrey?"

"Yes. What will your Mom say?"

"I already told her I suspected your baby was mine so she's going to be so happy to find out it's true. She's been bugging me a lot lately to make her a Grandma before she dies. Last night though I was afraid I wasn't going to be able to do that. But now touching your stomach makes me realize that life is exactly the way it should be. Just the way Mom has wanted it. Let's go tell her. It should make her day."

We head off to the clinic to see his mom and tell her the good news. Telling my family won't be as easy. My brothers are going to kill Maysen. Mom, Dad and the girls all know but the boys, not so much. I better hide Maysen when I do tell them. Or the baby and I will live without him forever. I shake my head at thought because there is no way I'm letting that happen again.

21

"Hi! How are you? Of course, I'll be right there!" I hang up my phone and turn to Maysen and his Mom.

"Everything okay? Where are you going?" he asks once I do.

"That's my best friend Tracey. She's in town for a few hours and wants me to meet her at Sally's. Do you mind if I go? I haven't seen her in a long time. I'll tell you the whole story later. You don't mind do you?" I walk up to Maysen and kiss him on the cheek and then do the same to his Mom.

"Of course not. Do you want me to drop you off? We did come in my car."

"Oh I forgot. No, I'll just walk there and let you know when I'm ready for a ride after. Will that work? I'm sorry to run off like this Martha."

"I am just so grateful you told Maysen about the baby. You two will be wonderful parents. Take care of yourself sweetheart."

"I will thank you. I'll see you soon. Bye Maysen. I'll call

you." I smile and walk out the door of her room. Once out of sight I stop and breathe in deep. Is this really happening? I'm getting the happily ever after? I look up to the Heavens and say a little prayer, that's all I can do.

****

"Hey man, just wanted to let you know that I'm going to be a father. Yep, Audrey and I talked today. Yep. I know it's a little strange to know that I'm going to have a son to take care of. Yep a son. I know it's so exciting. Why don't you come to Colvin for the weekend? I need help settling into my new house anyway. Awesome. See you then."

Carter's going to come and help me move. That way I can get the house done before Mom gets out of the hospital.

"Moving into Audrey's brother's house this weekend are you?"

"Yes we are. The second room will be perfect for you Ma."

"No son. I'm not moving into that house with you. You're going to have a family and I don't want to be in the way when that happens. I'll be just fine and happy with Ingrid and Sam."

"No you're coming with me. Audrey and I just reconciled things; we're not getting married today."

"Maysen I said no. You are not moving me into that house. It's not something I want to do. I want to stay with my sister and you need to have alone time right now."

"Ma. Why are you being difficult?"

"I am still your mother and this is what I want. When your son is born you can make all the decisions for him. But I am still perfectly capable of making my own decision of where I'm going to live. I appreciate your wanting to take care of me but I don't need you to. I know I haven't kept myself hydrated but I will be fine from now on. It scared the crazy right out of me. Promise."

"Fine. You seem to have your mind made up. I will still come check on you whenever I can."

"I count on it. And I count on your new girl coming with you."

"No doubt. I love you Ma. I need to get back to work though. See you later."

"Goodbye son. I love you. So very happy for you."

"I knew you would be. I am so happy I could burst." I kiss Mom goodbye and head back to the shop.

Once I get back to the shop I see that the Blake brothers are there. Oh boy. I guess I'm about to get what's coming to me now that they know I'm the loser who knocked up their sister. At least that's how they describe it.

"Hey guys! What's up?"

"We just came to see how your Mom was doing. Audrey isn't answering her phone right now so we thought we'd just swing by."

"Mom's great. She was pretty dehydrated. Thanks again for staying at the clinic with me. Much appreciated."

"The least we could do for a friend. But speaking of friends, when did you and our little sister get to be so chummy? I know you said she was just there at the right time, but she stayed by your side the whole time. It was just weird for barely knowing each other."

"She's just a nice girl that did a good thing."

"That she is. Well, glad to hear your Mom's okay." Austin says and motions for Austin to follow. I'm not sure if they bought that line or if their still wondering about us.

****

"Hey Tracey! How are you? Oh my goodness it's so good to see you! I've missed you so much!" I fly into her open arms the minute I get into Sally's.

"Oh my goodness looks like we have a lot to catch up on! How far along are you? Who's the lucky man?"

"Oh yeah I guess there is. I'm in the third trimester and feeling actually pretty good. His name is Maysen. How are you? How long are you here for?"

"Only the weekend. I was hoping to spend most of it with you but maybe I'll have to share you."

"No, I'll try to spend all the time I can with you. I'm so happy to see you."

"Thank you for being so nice to me after what I did to you and your family. That was inexcusable."

"We all know it was the addiction that was in charge of your life at that time. I take it you're clean?"

"Yes. I couldn't touch that stuff again if I had to. It did such terrible things to me or I did those terrible things. The guilt was the toughest thing to get over. Sometimes I'm not entirely sure I'm over it though."

"Well we don't hold any of that against you. Don't worry about that. Are you staying at the hotel?"

"Yes. I didn't figure staying with you on the ranch would have been a good idea."

"It would have been fine. So, what are your plans now that you're clean and on the right path?"

"I'm working in Tulsa actually at an outreach program. I

help those who have addictions get the help they need. It's amazing being able to give back."

"Tracey that is amazing! I am so proud of you."

"Thanks. So, tell me all about everyone. What's been going on besides you getting prego?"

"Aiden and Karlie got married and had a baby girl named Aleah. Austin met Leah and they're engaged too. Mom and Dad are the same. Not really much other than that!"

"That's a lot Audrey! I am so thankful Karlie stuck by Aiden's side after I did what I did to them. I'll never be able to apologize enough to them. Do they know I'm here?"

"Actually Karlie was with me when you called the other day. She said she's fine with you being back. She doesn't hold anything against you either."

"She really is an amazing woman. Such a kind heart. How's your Mom doing with being a Grandma? I bet she's the best."

"She is. Aleah has her wrapped around her little finger and she's very excited about her first grandson here." I say and pat my stomach.

"A boy huh? Wow I'm so excited for you. Tell me everything."

I start at the beginning and once again tell the Maysen and Audrey tale. Last time I told it I wasn't sure it was going to end with happily ever after, but this time I feel it will.

****

"Hey. I'm staying at Tracey's room at the hotel tonight. Could you bring me my bag from my car?" I hear Audrey say when I answer my phone.

"Sure. I'll bring the car to the hotel for you. You doing okay?"

"I'm perfect Maysen. I have everything and everyone I could ever want. I just haven't seen her in so long and she's only here for the weekend."

"I get it. Carter's coming tonight too. He's going to help me get all settled into Austin's house. Speaking of Austin, he and Aiden stopped by the shop earlier wondering about us and where you were. We really need to tell them before they hear it from someone else."

"I'll call the girls and have them tell the guys. That way neither of us loses our lives! Haha just kidding."

"Not funny at all. I was so nervous around them today I was afraid they were there to murder me. Anyway, I'll bring your car in a minute. See you in a few."

"Thank you. See you in a few." I'm a little disappointed that I won't have her all to myself tonight after we just sort of reconciled today, but she misses her friend like I miss Carter I suppose.

I drive Audrey's car to the hotel and wait to find out which room she's in. I am about to call her when I see her come out of a room up on the second floor and smile when she sees me. Watching her walk down the stairs and across the parking lot towards me has my heart racing and I pray, "God I thank you for such a wonderful person. I thank you for bringing her back to me. Amen."

I can't help but smile back after my little prayer. My heart is so full of love right now I might need medical attention.

"Hey there. Thanks for bringing my car. Wanna come up and meet Tracey?"

"You're welcome. Sure, if you want me to." I get out of the car and follow her up the stairs.

Once we reach the top she pauses to allow me to walk beside

her and she takes my hand in hers. The feeling of her skin against mine makes my stomach do somersaults. Just her slight touch sends me in a tail spin. I still can't believe she's here beside me again.

"Tracey, this is Maysen. Maysen, my best friend since childhood Tracey."

We both say our nice to meet you's and shake hands. She is not what I had pictured. She is a very pretty woman but nothing compared to Audrey.

"So, you're the elusive baby daddy are ya?" Tracey says and laughs.

"I guess so yes. Didn't realize you had enough time to tell her the gruesome details." I look at Audrey questioning why she had to tell her all of it. She smiles at me and I realize that I told Carter too so I can't really say much. Pot calling the kettle black I guess.

"Don't worry I know it was because you two were idiots and didn't get phone numbers. Sure glad you got your what? Third chance?"

"Third time's a charm right? Isn't that what they say?" Audrey puts her arm around my waist and leans her head on my chest. I can't help but sigh and kiss the top of her head.

"I'll take it. Well, I better let you two get caught up. Carter my buddy from Tulsa should be here soon too. If you two get bored you can come help us move my stuff around in Austin's house. Well you can sit and watch." I smile and lay my hand on Audrey's stomach hoping to feel my son kick again.

"Protective already? Wow. We'll see you later. I'll walk you out. Be right back Tracey."

Walking to the stairs I try to reach for her hand but she's slightly behind me and I can't reach it. I stop at the stairs and turn around to face her.

"What's wrong? You're quiet all of a sudden."

"I don't want you to leave. I just found you again. Her timing was not very good for us."

"Audrey, I'm here forever. She's only here for a day or so. I'll still be here when she isn't. I've waited for six months for this, a couple more days isn't going to kill me. Go, have fun. I'll see you later. Okay?" I put my finger under her chin and raise her face to me. I could look into this face all day long and never get tired of it. Even when she's pouting like a child.

"I'll hold you to that. We will hold you to that." She takes my hands and rests them on her stomach. Just as she does that the baby decides to do gymnastics. We both smile at each other and I'm finally able to kiss her again. All is right with the world.

****

Maysen's lips touching mine feels like Heaven. My heart is full of love and happiness. I can't believe it's all real. This hunk of a man in front of me is definitely my Prince Charming and the man of my dreams.

"I love you Audrey. I don't ever want you to doubt that."

"I love you too Maysen. I don't want you to ever doubt that either."

"Never again. Now go, have your girl time and I'll see you later." He releases me to go but I don't move. He turns me around by my shoulders and gives me a gentle push. I then start to walk away but turn back around and walk backwards.

"Have fun moving. I'll be dreaming of you tonight."

"And I of you. Always do. Have a good night Audrey." He walks down the stairs but looks back up at me and sees me still standing at the railing watching him go. I wave and blow him a kiss which he returns. I love that man with all of my heart.

22

The next morning Tracey and I decide to have breakfast at Sally's. We drive over in my car and walk in the door. Sally greets us as we walk in. I can tell Tracey's a little timid and not sure how her being back is going to be perceived by some.

"Well Miss Tracey Wheeler! It's so good to see you hon!" Sally yells and wraps Tracey up in a big hug. I can see the relief on Tracey's face as she does. I smile at her and hope she starts to heal a little more inside. She might have done terrible things but she's a changed person and wants to make things right.

"See I told you we all loved you around here." I smile and walk to the only booth open this morning. I should have known the place would be busy. Sally's Café is the best place to eat any time of day. I sit down and start to scour the menu because I'm starving. This baby is starving all the time.

"Starving? You look like you're about to eat the menu."

"Hey be nice! I can't help it if this kid wants to eat all the time." We laugh and finally decide on what we are going to have.

"I'll be right back with your drinks girls. So good to have you back again Tracey dear."

"I won't say I told you so."

"You just did."

"Hey, isn't that your Prince Charming over there?"

I look out the window to see Maysen getting out of his car and another man out of the other side. I've never seen this guy before so he must be Carter.

I wait for him to look up and see us through the window and when he does my stomach does flip flops. Or maybe the baby just knows his daddy is near. I wave big to him and smile while he returns them. The other guy with him just shakes his head and rolls his eyes. Definitely Carter.

"Hey, how are you this morning? Get all moved in last night?" I ask Maysen once they get inside and come to our booth.

After he leans down and gives me a quick kiss he replies, "Yep. Just have to finish putting it all away now."

"Wanna join us? You don't mind do you Tracey?" I look at my friend who I catch looking at Maysen's friend like she could eat him for breakfast.

"Not. At. All. Please sit down." She slides to the wall of the booth allowing the guy to sit down next to her but slips closer once he does. I give her a stern look but she just smiles back. It's so good to have her back.

"Audrey and Tracey this is my friend Carter. Carter, Audrey and Tracey."

"So nice to meet you! Thanks for coming and helping Maysen move."

"Nice to finally put a face to the name. I've heard so much about you over the past several months. Congrats on the baby too."

"Thank you. I couldn't be happier. It's a boy did you know that?"

"WE couldn't be happier." Maysen says and pulls me closer to his side and kisses my temple. I look up at him and smile.

"I think I heard that fact at some point or another." He smiles mischievously at Maysen. So that tells me he's been filled in too.

"So he knows all the details too huh?"

"Every bit of it. Even why he was late getting to the house last night. You know I had to sit there in the driveway for half an hour until this fool came walking up."

"I'm sorry about that. My fault entirely."

"Yeah I'm sure you twisted his arm. Anyway, what are you two having? I'm starved. This guy has nothing in his house to eat."

"Dude, I just moved in. Haven't had time to go to the grocery store."

"Yeah, looks like you've been busy all right." Carter motions to me and we all laugh knowing his meaning. I redden a little too but see that Maysen is even redder than I.

We all ate and enjoyed each other's company for an hour or so. It was so nice to have Maysen's friend and my friend there with us. More than anything it was great to have Maysen there beside me.

****

Goodness I love this woman. I can't believe I get to kiss and touch her. I really need to be alone with her though for a little while at least. I need to make sure she and I are on the same page here. I don't want to get ahead of myself if she isn't ready for forever. I'll go buy a ring tomorrow when the stores open if she's ready for that.

"Well, I think I'm going to head back to Tulsa. I have a lot of work to get done before tomorrow. Will you walk me out Audrey? It was so nice to meet both of you gentlemen. Take good care of my girl here will you?"

"No need to ask that. I will do anything for her. It was great to meet you. We should all get together again sometime. Have a safe trip."

"I'll be right back." Audrey kisses my cheek and walks out with her friend. I can't help but feel excited that she's going to be alone. Now I just need to get rid of Carter without offending him.

"I suppose you want me to leave too so you can be alone with your sweet thing?"

"You read my mind. I didn't know how to say it without hurting your feelings."

"Nah, I have people to see anyway, I'll be on my way too. Walk me out?" He says with the same tone that Tracey had asked Audrey.

"Haha you're a funny man. I appreciate you coming and helping."

"Anytime. Keep me updated on what's happening here. Maybe one day I'll be ready to settle down too and come back. Right now I have ladies waiting." We hug and say goodbye. I'm actually going to miss this idiot but excited to be alone with Audrey.

Once I get out the doors with Carter I see that Audrey has said her goodbyes and Tracey's pulling away. She looks at me with such emotion on her face that it hits me straight in my chest. This girl really does feel the same as me.

"All set? Can I get a ride to my house?" She nods and we head to her car.

"It was so good to see Tracey. One day I need to tell you the whole sorted tale about her but right now I just can't wait to get you alone. And naked."

"Whoa Miss Blake are you trying to seduce me?"

"Whatever it takes to get you to make love to me again. I have been waiting for months."

"What about the baby? Won't that hurt him?"

"No. He'll be fine. Doctor said it was fine too."

"When do you go again? I want to go with you from now on. Can I?"

"Of course you can. That would be nice if you would go."

"Nice? I'll show you what nice is once I get you in my bedroom."

"Why Maysen you wouldn't trap me in a room with no chance of escape would you?"

"You won't want to exit anytime soon Miss Blake. You are going to be busy all day long." About this time we pull up in my driveway and I bail out of the car and rush to her side. As soon as she steps out I lift her up and run to my bedroom as quick as my feet could take us. I have dreamed of this happening since the morning in the hotel room. I am not letting this day go by without making love to Audrey again. And again.

"I love you so much Maysen." I murmur my sentiments back but can't make myself think of anything but getting closer to Audrey. Getting as close as I possibly can be.

****

"Answer the door Maysen. We know she's in there!" We hear banging on the door later that evening. We both startle awake and smile knowing if her brothers were to get in that door they would not like what we just did. Three times.

"I better go talk to them first. The girls must have filled them in on the paternity of our son." She gets out of bed and dresses as quick as she can before her brothers knock down the front door.

"I'll be right there too. Better to face this head on than be a coward."

"You have no idea what you're getting yourself into. But I love you anyway." She leans over and kisses me.

"Go get the door before I no longer have one." I pat her on the butt and she heads out to face the firing squad.

"Calm down you two idiots. The neighbors don't need to hear you acting stupid." She says as she reaches the door. Unlocking it and stepping back I see her brothers come bailing through it searching all around for me. Once they catch sight of me coming in the room they both step towards me. But before they can get too far Audrey steps in front of them. The look on her face stops them dead in their tracks.

"If you take one more step towards him I will give you each a black eye. Do you hear me?"

"Audrey we're going to kill him." Austin says and takes another step. Before any of us sees it coming, she punches him directly in the right eye.

"I warned you! Leave him alone. Aiden?" She just punched her brother. For me. Wow that's sexy and completely stupid. They're really going to want to murder me now.

"What the hell are you doing here Audrey? He knocked you up and left you." Aiden booms out while shooting daggers my way. He isn't stupid enough to take that step he was warned not to take though.

"I'm a big girl and I can make my own damned choices. I have been telling you that for years. You were told the whole story and you know it. Maysen didn't even know about the baby. I couldn't tell him. But now that he does know he's here. Here with me. Or I'm here with him, whatever. Deal with it."

"I love your sister with all my heart. I'm over the moon excited about becoming a father. I promise you I didn't know this was my baby but now that I do I will never ever let her be alone."

"And you believe this hogwash?" Austin says gesturing towards me.

"Every word. You two had rocky roads with the loves of your lives. Maysen and I have had ours. But we are together now. I love you two so much for wanting to protect me but you don't need to protect me from Maysen."

"You're sure?" Aiden asks one more time but looks to be calming down. Thank goodness.

"More than anything. I love Maysen and want to spend the rest of my life with him and our son."

I take that opportunity to walk up behind Audrey. I'm not sure I heard her right. So I reach out and turn her slightly my way. "You do? You want to spend the rest of your life with me?"

"Of course I do silly. You're my everything. I don't want to ever be separated from you again."

"Thank God." I wrap her in my arms and before I remember that her brothers are here we feel them retreat. They take this moment as proof of what my intentions are with their baby sister. We look up to see them walk out the door and both smile at us before shutting the door.

"Whew that was close. I can't believe you hit your brother."

"I've done it before. I'll do it again too if they threaten you anymore."

"I love you Slugger." I kiss her again and carry her back to the bedroom. I don't anticipate any more interruptions today.

23

"My family wants to have a barbeque tonight and you're invited. They all want to meet you. Well, meet you as my guy and my baby's father." I say and kiss Maysen on the nose.

"Your guy huh? Is that the same as boyfriend? Or just a guy friend?"

"My everything. Boyfriend doesn't do justice to the feelings I have for you."

"Do you want to get married before our son is born?"

"Oh my goodness Maysen are you serious? Of course I would love to marry you! That wasn't your proposal was it?"

"No Slugger, I was just asking if you were interested in marrying me. I would want nothing more than for you to be my wife when our son is brought into this world."

I squeal and jump into Maysen's arms. "I want nothing more than that too!"

"Ok well now that we're all on the same page I can start planning the proposal."

"It doesn't have to be a big deal Maysen. We've already conceived a child before marriage."

"I still have to ask your father for permission before I can ask you. If we'll be around him tonight I can ask him then." He smiles and gets up to shower for the barbeque. I love this man so much and now we're going to get married someday? Be still my heart.

I put my hands on my stomach and say to my son, "Did you hear that little man? Your daddy wants to marry us."

****

"Are you sure they'll all be okay with me being here?" I ask for probably the hundredth time since we left my house.

"Maysen stop worrying. This is all their idea. They want to get to know you better."

"Or kill me and bury me somewhere on this humongous ranch where no one will ever find me." I look out the car window and see the vast expanse of land Audrey's family owns. It seems to go on forever.

"Don't be silly. They'll love you as much as I do. Besides everyone has loved you since you came to town."

"Maybe but that's before we all found out about the baby and Omaha."

"My brothers didn't hurt you earlier today so I can promise you no one else will either. Just relax."

"That's easy for you to say. They love you already."

"And I love you so quit acting like a girl." She laughs and smiles.

"Okay maybe I am being a bit of a girl but dangit I'm

nervous. I am meeting my future in-laws for the first time, that's not an easy thing to swallow."

"Baby just try to relax. We aren't part of the Mafia or anything."

"That might be easier. At least then I would know what they're capable of."

"Maysen shut up already. We're here anyway. Breathe. It's going to be fine. I'll be here to protect you if you need it."

"Why are they all coming out of the house? Couldn't they wait to kill me when I got inside?" I see all the Blakes filing out of the house and standing around like a mob of angry people. Holy crap what have I gotten myself into.

"Relax honey. It's okay." She reaches for my hand and we walk towards the crowd of Maysen haters. I try to breathe in deep and exhale but I'm already holding my breath.

"Hey guys, this is Maysen. But you already know that." She shoves me forward towards the men who I see have the worst expressions on their faces. I gulp and try to smile.

"Welcome Maysen. So glad you could make it." AJ says then her brothers say the same. I must be dreaming. I think they knocked me out and I'm dreaming that things went so well. I look around for Audrey but she's walking in the door with the women leaving me to fend for myself. So much for she'll be here to protect me.

"Thank you for inviting me."

"Before we go inside we need to get a few things off of our chests." AJ says and steps in front of the boys and closer to me.

"First of all I'm sorry you didn't know about the baby until recently. Second, we hope you'll make our Audrey as happy for the rest of her life as she is right now."

I freeze and stare at the man in front of me. He didn't hit me; he didn't say terrible things to me. He is accepting me and sorry about me not knowing? Seriously? I have to be dreaming.

"We know you love our sister and that she loves you." Aiden says from behind his father.

"We wish you two the best." Austin then chimes in. He really has a shiner brought on by his little sister.

"I don't really know what to say. I was expecting you guys to murder me and bury me out in one of your pastures."

"Nah, Audrey would do the same with us anyway." AJ chuckles and slaps me on the shoulder.

"Come on son, let's go get a drink."

"Um sir, I'd like to talk to you about something before we do."

"Sure, go on ahead boys we'll be right in. I'm sure your sister is worried to death in there. Go assure her he's alive." He chuckles and puts an arm around my shoulders which then guides us to a couple of chairs nearby.

"Sir."

"Please call me AJ. No need for formalities anymore."

"AJ I was hoping that I could ask you for permission to marry your daughter."

"I was praying you would say that. Of course you have my permission. You two need to get it done soon though. You have very little time left if you want her to have your last name when she delivers that little boy."

"Yes, I want that so much. Thank you for your permission. If it's also okay with you, I'd like to ask her tonight at the barbeque."

"That would be great. Welcome to the family Maysen. You'll forever be one of my sons too."

"Thank you so much. That means the world to me."

****

"Please tell me you two didn't pummel him."

"No sis. He's out there talking to Dad right now. He'll be back in soon. Relax."

"You're okay with us now? Wait, he's talking to Dad alone?" I smile.

"Yes Aud. You love him and he loves you. End of story."

"No, beginning of the story you idiot!" I pretend to punch Aiden in the stomach and he grabs my hands and hugs me instead.

"We're happy for you sis. Be happy." Austin says and hugs me too.

"I am and I always will be as long as I have Maysen."

"Hey we understand. Now if we could just get Austin and Leah to set a date we might all be happy." Aiden punches Austin in the shoulder.

"We have you idiot. We're going to tell you all tonight." I smile and hug Austin again.

"YAY!! I can't wait to help plan another wedding."

"Well, you might be planning your own sometime soon." We all turn around to see Mom come up behind us with a big sweet smile on her face.

"Let's not rush it Mama. We just found each other again. We'll get married someday."

THIRD TIME'S A CHARM

"I know sweet girl, I know. Dinner's ready. Where are Maysen and your Daddy?"

"Out front still." I give Mom a strange look and decide it's time to rescue my man.

"Hey Daddy. Maysen. Mama says it's time to eat."

"Come here baby girl." I walk into Dad's waiting arms. He kisses me on the top of my head like he always has and I feel his love for me. The love I'll have for my son and Maysen will have for our son too.

"Love you Daddy." Dad hands me off to Maysen and walks into the house.

"You're still standing. Told you." I smile and look down at his hands resting on the baby.

"It was a tough battle but I came out victorious." He raises his hand up in the victory pose. What a goof.

"I can't believe you just did that! Let's go eat. Your son is starving!" I kiss him and pull him into the house and out to the back porch.

****

"I want to thank you all for inviting me out here and being so accepting of me and Audrey. I know things weren't actually done conventionally but I promise from this day forward we will do things by the book. Starting with this." I kneel down on one knee in front of Audrey who has a surprised look on her face.

"Audrey Blake, will you make me the happiest and blessed man in the whole world and agree to be my wife? My son and I would like nothing more than for us to be a proper family. I love you and our son so much. What do you say? Will you marry me?"

Audrey just sits there with her hand over her mouth. The

179

longer she sits there the more worried I am that she really isn't ready for this. Then she stands up and kneels down in front of me taking my hands. She's seriously going to turn me down in front of all of her family. I breathe in deep and exhale. This is going to hurt.

"Maysen Michael Correli you are the most amazing person I have ever met. I know you're going to be the best father to our son. Just like the one that my brothers and I have. Getting married is such a big commitment and having a son all at once isn't right either. I will marry you on one condition."

I hear everyone gasp as she finally says the yes part. My heart was about the break into a million pieces. Wait? One condition?

"What condition Slugger?"

"We do it tonight. We can call Reverend Lowell and he could marry us tonight."

"Audrey that was not what I thought you were going to say. I honestly thought you were going to turn me down."

"I could never say no to a lifetime with you Maysen. Mom? Dad? Could you get things figured out with Reverend Lowell? We need to go get Martha. She needs to be here to witness her only child getting married. Right?" She says and looks at me with an abundance of love and excitement.

"Yes baby yes. Let's go. I love you by the way. Have I told you that lately?"

"Every ten minutes. You know you sounded like a love song there don't you?"

"I don't care. That's how I feel. Let's go get my Mom. We're getting married tonight!" I wrap my arms around my bride-to-be and kiss her with all the feeling I have inside me.

"I love you Maysen. Did you really think I was going to say

no?"

"No but you weren't exactly screaming yes. Everyone else gasped too when you finally said you would."

"I'm sorry to scare you like that. I want to spend the rest of my life waking up beside you and going to sleep beside you."

"And a little bit in between there I hope?" I wiggle my eyebrows at her making her giggle with delight.

"Always. Hurry up so we can get back and get married!!"

24

"Everything is set. Reverend will be here in about an hour. I think Karlie and Leah have something for you in your apartment. They'll help you get ready and I'll be up there in a minute. Maysen you come with me and I'll show you to a room where you can change too." Amelia says to us once we walk back into their house with my mother.

"Oh I never thought about what I was wearing. I don't even own a suit."

"Austin's got one for you to borrow. They're all in the guest bedroom down the hall. It's the third door on your right. Martha, if you'll come with me I could really use your help setting things up."

"Of course. This is all so sudden and so exciting. I'll be in there to see you before it all starts Maysen."

"Ok, see you in a few Ma. Thank you so much Amelia."

"You're going to be a part of our family very soon. It's what we do for family. You need to go get changed. My daughter is going to be expecting her groom to be ready."

"Yes ma'am. Thank you again." I turn around and walk down the hallway with so much excitement it takes all the self-control I have not to jump up and click my heels together.

Third door on the right. Ah here it is and of course Aiden and Austin are both inside looking dashing. I hope I can look half as good for my bride. I can't wait to see how beautiful she is. I bet she'll look like an angel.

****

"Karlie? Leah? Mom said you two were in here. Hello?" I walk through my apartment looking for the two of them.

"We're in your bedroom!" I hear Karlie yell so I cautiously walk to my room. What in the world are they doing in my room?

"What are you two doing?" I walk in my room and see them scurrying around like little elves. They have dresses and shoes strewn all over my bedroom.

"We're finding your wedding dress you goof. You didn't give us much time to get one! Next time please don't give us an hour's notice before a wedding! Now get undressed."

"I was just going to wear my white maternity dress I got for the summer months. It'll work just fine."

"It would have been fine yes. But you have to be stunning! So, we've found a few different things in your closet and ours that we've taken apart and created a fabulous one of a kind wedding dress for you! Isn't it gorgeous?" Leah says and holds up their creation.

"That is the most beautiful wedding dress I think I have ever seen. How did you two pull this off?" I can't believe they did this. The dress is fitted everywhere above the waist and flowing below.

"This bottom part is from my wedding dress. Recognize it? I took out the stitches and just attached it to the bottom of the dress you already had. With it being a maternity dress we knew it would fit you. So we built on that."

"Karlie, you took that off of your own wedding dress? Won't you miss it? How could you trash your own like that? Leah why did you let her do that?"

"Actually I took some off my Grandmother's dress I found in the attic. The lace veil is hers too. We want you to have the most beautiful wedding we can throw for you. It makes us happy to do this. Just be thankful and go with it."

"Girls I can't believe you have both done this. I can't begin to tell you how much it means to me. Is the dress all done?"

"All ready for your hot body to get inside of it. Do you want your hair up or down?" Karlie asks and gestures for me to come put the dress on. I slip out of the dress I was currently wearing and step out of my sandals.

"We have shoes for you too. Remember the little slippers we got for all of you bridesmaids at our wedding? We found yours in the bottom of your closet and those will be perfect and comfy under your dress. You'll never see them either."

"You two are amazing and I love you so much! You're exactly the sisters I always wanted!!"

"We love you too. Now hurry up and get in that chair so I can do your hair and makeup. The clock is ticking and you're going to have a handsome groom down there waiting patiently to see you look beautiful." Leah says and gets busy with my makeup and hair brush.

"I can't believe I'm marrying the man of my dreams in a few minutes. This is so surreal."

"You're the one who said it had to be tonight. Whatever possessed you to do it so soon?"

"What? Should I wait as long as you and Austin have?"

"Actually we were going to tell you all at dinner that we had set a date for the wedding but you and Prince Charming kinda stole the show." Leah stood there smiling with her hand on her hip.

"OH!! I'm so sorry. When is it?"

"October 6th."

"Of this year right??" Karlie pipes up.

"Of course. We've waited long enough. You two can start planning tomorrow. Tonight it's all about your special day Audrey! I am so overly happy for you and Maysen."

"Leah I am so thankful to have you in our lives too. Austin has been such a changed person since you came back. And Karlie, we all know you and Aiden never could have stayed apart. I have the sweetest niece and I'm so thankful for what you two are doing and have done for me."

"No crying. This makeup will run and then you'll look like the Bride of Chucky." Leah growls making us all bust out laughing.

"Can I join the pre-party?" We turn to see my Mom peeking in the doorway of my bedroom smiling and wearing the dress she wore for Aiden and Karlie's wedding. She looks so young and beautiful in it.

"Of course you can Mom. Is Maysen ready? And Martha? Did she get a good spot to sit?"

"Yes honey everyone is ready and waiting for the bride. I just wanted to tell you how proud I am of the woman you have become and of the man you have chosen to marry. Maysen is wonderful and his mother is also a wonderful woman. When Aiden married Karlie I gained a daughter and a very good friend in her mother. I will gain another son and a friend in his mother tonight also. I love you girls so much. Let's go make you a Mrs." Mom hugs each one of us leaving me for last because we all know with these hormones I'm going to need a touchup on my makeup.

"I love you so much Mom. I will strive to be a mother like you have been to me and my brothers. You're the most amazing woman I know and am so blessed to have you as my mother. My son will be blessed to have you as one of his two amazing grandmothers."

"Okay let's fix the makeup and blow this popsicle stand!" Karlie blurts out and we all laugh until we almost cry.

****

"May I come in?" I hear a familiar voice from the doorway of the room we're getting ready in. I turn around to see my mother's smiling face. She looks so full of pride and happiness tonight. It's so very good to see her like that again. She's been so sick in recent years that it's been tough to be too happy.

"Of course you can Ma. Is my tie crooked? This stupid bowtie is choking me. The guys think this is what Audrey would want me to wear so I'm wearing it. Even though I have never worn a penguin suit in my life, I'll wear it for my bride whenever she wants." I smile and at my mom and she starts to tear up.

"Maysen I am so proud of you. You have found your true love and will be marrying her tonight. You'll soon be a father and I know with all my heart you'll be the best husband and father anyone could ask for. I have worked so hard over the years to ensure you were the kind of man a woman would want and now that you are I couldn't be happier." She hugs me and I feel her sob while in my arms.

"Ma don't cry. You're going to mess up that makeup Audrey did for you and I'm going to cry too. I love you and you've been the best mother any guy could ask for. My son will be so blessed to have you and Amelia as his Grandmothers. I love you. Thank you for teaching me to be a man and to be a good one."

"Knock knock. Mom says it's time. You ready for this?" Aiden asks from the doorway now. I look at mom's smiling face and then at Aiden's. This really is happening. I'm going to marry the girl of my dreams. Tonight. Right now. Wow!

"More than ready. Let's go." I motion for Mom to follow Aiden and I follow her down the hallway and out onto the back patio.

25

I'm struck with how amazing the backyard looks. This place has transformed into the most spectacular outdoor wedding. White lights twinkle in the trees. Chairs are set up facing a gazebo that's adorned with white lights and white roses all over. I don't know how much of the yard looks like this year round but it's amazing. It's better than anything I could ever have dreamed up myself. Mom and I walk down the aisle to the front where I see a man who must be Reverend Lowell. I shake his hand and thank him for being here on such short notice. I walk my mother to her seat in the front row. And Carter's here too. Wow.

"Hey man, what's up? How did you get here so fast?"

"I was actually still here. I'll tell you about that later. You look pretty sharp!"

"I'm so glad to have my best friend here with me when I marry Audrey."

"Of course man. Don't worry about it. When you go big you go really big don't you? A son and wife all in a couple of days." Carter jokes and slaps me on the back.

"Hey, when it's right it's right." I smile and take my place at the front. I look around and see everyone I know here. Aunt Ingrid and Uncle Sam are sitting with Mom. Amelia's sitting on the other side with an empty chair for AJ. Aiden and Karlie with Aleah and Austin with Leah. Even Tracey made it? That's interesting. How did she and Carter both get back here so quickly? Anyway, most everyone I have met from the garage is here too. Audrey must know the rest because I think that's the extent of those that I do.

I can't keep this foolish grin off my face. I am so over the moon happy to be marrying Audrey tonight. I can't wait to look her in the eyes and tell her I want to spend the rest of our lives together. Now's my chance. The wedding march starts playing. And oh my goodness there is the most gorgeous woman I have ever laid eyes on. And she's about to become my wife. What did I do to deserve this? "Thank you Jesus for bringing her to me."

****

"It's time baby girl. Are you ready?" Dad asks me as he lowers my veil over my face.

"More ready than I have ever been for anything in my life Daddy. I love you. Let's go I can't wait to see my groom." We start to walk towards the back doors of the house. Mom set it all up out in the back yard. Oh my goodness that's exactly what we had talked about so much while I was growing up. She remembered almost every detail.

"Oh Daddy it looks so beautiful."

"Your Mama has always planned on doing this for you sweetheart. She never forgot all those nights you two dreamed it all up."

"I'm going to cry again." I try to breathe and not cry. I can't cry until after the pictures at least. Speaking of pictures I look around for Karlie. There she is camera in hand.

"Don't cry now. Your old man here doesn't wanna look like a sap in front of everyone." He smiles down at me and I'm finally at ease. This is all right and perfect. I look up to where I see Maysen standing waiting for me at the end of the pathway. I tighten my hold on Dad's arm as we step down the patio steps and onto the grass. In between rows of chairs we walk step by step getting me closer to my Prince Charming.

"Who gives this woman to be married tonight?" Reverend Lowell asks as we reach the end of the pathway. I turn to my father and then to my mother who has stood up on my other side. "Her mother and I do." Daddy gives me a kiss on the forehead and Mama gives me a kiss on the cheek. She smiles so big I know it has to be hurting. I love seeing her and everyone else so happy. They look as happy as I am.

I feel Maysen's hand slip in mine as we step forward and face each other in front of the Reverend. "We are gathered here today in front of God and all of you to join Maysen and Audrey in holy matrimony."

Maysen and I look at each other and as soon as our eyes lock I'm honestly not sure what else the Reverend said or how long we stood there entranced in each other.

We both jump back into reality in time to hear, "Maysen repeat after me." Sure hope we didn't miss anything else too important. I hope Karlie's videoing this too so I can watch it later to see what all was said. That makes me giggle a little and from the look on Maysen's face he's thinking the same thing.

"Audrey, today I take you as my wife. I promise to love you without reservation, comfort you in times of distress, encourage you to achieve all of your goals, laugh with you and cry with you, grow with you in mind and spirit, always be open and honest with you, and cherish you for as long as we both shall live."

As the perfect man recites his vow to me I can't help but let a few tears fall. I start shaking and it's getting too hard to fight off the emotion any more. Mom must have seen it coming because she stood up and handed me a tissue just as I was about to lose it.

190

Maysen also saw it coming and squeezed my hands tighter and smiled at me. I took a deep breath and exhaled. That's better. Whew I almost lost it there. That would have been embarrassing.

I say my vow to Maysen as eloquently as he did to me. Once again it's the Reverend's turn but this time I make sure I pay attention to his words. One of these times he's going to say you can kiss your bride and I'm not missing that part.

"If anyone here has any reason that these two shouldn't be joined in holy matrimony, speak now or forever hold your peace." We look at each and then at the Reverend while both of us are thinking let's move on. Get to the pronounce you man and wife stuff.

"Then by the power vested in me by God above and the State of Oklahoma, I pronounce you man and wife. Maysen you may kiss your bride."

You didn't have to tell Maysen twice on that part. Before I could even process it he had my face in between his hands and pressing his lips to mine. Sealing the vows and making me his and him mine for eternity. I kiss him back with every part of my being. This is my husband. The only man I will ever want to kiss until the day I die.

"I love you so much Audrey. We did it. We're married." He says and twirls me around.

"I love you too Maysen. Let's get some cake. I'm starved again!" Everyone cracks up laughing that heard me say the cake part. Great that wasn't supposed to come out that loud. But oh well, this is my wedding after all.

"I now present to you, Mr. and Mrs. Maysen Correli."

We start on down the aisle stopping to get congratulations from everyone. I'm just so happy I could implode. From the look on Maysen's face he feels the same.

26

We did it. She's my wife. I have a wife and I couldn't be more happy and proud. She's the most beautiful woman I've ever laid eyes on. That baby inside her stomach makes the deal even sweeter.

We stop to sign the marriage license and it's officially official. I just married the woman of my dreams. Married. If you would have told me that last week or even four days ago I wouldn't have believed it. I am so thankful Audrey was put on this Earth to love me for eternity. I know I will love her that long. Maybe longer.

"Mrs. Correli are you ready to get that cake?" I wrap my arms around her from behind and lay my hands on her ever growing stomach. I feel our son move about that exact time and realize he's happy too that his parents just got hitched.

"More than you know!" She shrieks and we head for the cake table. With such short notice there sure is a wonderful assortment of cupcakes on this table. Every one of them had a C on them. Audrey's last name is Correli. It just dawned on me that she's got my last name now. What idiot doesn't think about that until now? Me I guess. I smile and look around at all the family and friends that are gathered around us. This is definitely a night we will never forget.

"I am so happy for you two. Maysen, you take care of my bestie here and make her as happy every day as she is today." Tracey says as she hugs Audrey.

"I will do just that. Thank you. I'm going to go talk to Carter for a few minutes. Enjoy my wife while I'm gone. I will be back to claim her soon." I kiss Audrey on the forehead and walk off towards my bestie. Good grief I'm already sounding like a girl. I smile knowing that I will see Audrey every day and every night for the rest of my life.

"Hey man, what's up? You ready to tell me now why you were close enough to Colvin to get here for the wedding? I'm not complaining or anything, it just weird. When you left this morning you said you were headed home." I lift an eyebrow which makes Carter crack up.

"Nothing gets by you does it Dude? If you and the Mrs. hadn't have decided last minute to get married you would never have known the difference. Do I really need to get into this now? Don't you need to run off into the sunset with your bride now?"

"No. Spill it." I cross my arms and wait for the details I'm not sure I'm going to like.

"I was with Tracey. At her hotel room." I immediately reach for his neck but he's quicker and I guess saw it coming.

"What the hell do you mean you were with Tracey? She's Audrey's best friend and has been through hell. The last thing she needs right now is a player like you messing with her plans. What were you thinking? Actually I know what you were thinking."

"Hey now, Mr. Judgmental. Chill out a minute. Nothing happened if that's what you're so pissed off about. We've been hanging out and just talking. She's so great to talk to. She even made me realize just how screwed up my priorities are."

"She did that in a few hours' time? I've been trying to do

that for YEARS!"

"I know Maysen but I like her. She's a very nice person and I loved spending time with her. I never even thought about jumping her bones. Promise."

"Oh my goodness I never thought I would hear those words come out of your mouth. I always thought you would be the seventy year old playboy."

"Hey now. You just got married not me. I didn't say I was cured, just that I see how bad my choices have been."

"Am I shocked to hear these words coming out of your mouth? Oh yes. Am I thankful someone finally made you see the light? Oh yes. But my wife's best friend who has had a crappy last couple of years? Dude really? You had better not hurt her. My wife will castrate you if you do. I promise you that."

"Wow. So much love coming my way. I promise Dude I won't hurt her. We're just friends. Good grief I only met her today. We're not running off into the sunset hand in hand like you. Chill out. No harm done, I promise. You go run along and find the ol' ball and chain. I'll deal with my own life thanks." Carter says and slaps me on the back. I nod and turn around in search of Audrey. Right now I would rather see her than deal with all of Carter's demons. That's his cross to bear right now, not mine. I just married an angel and I intend to keep her as happy as she is right now. But when she finds out about Carter she's going to kill us both.

****

"Could we have your attention please? Leah and I have an announcement of our own to make since we're all gathered in one spot for some a happy occasion." Austin says as he clinks the side of his glass. He reaches one arm around Leah and they both smile at each other.

"We have set a wedding date. We all want you to mark your calendars for October 6th. I'm sure the women will start the planning in the morning."

"Be nice son, we've been waiting a long time for this chance."

"Yes Ma, we have been. No more waiting, we're making it official in October."

"That's not very much time to get it all planned brother."

"Yes dear but you gave everyone a couple of hours."

"Touché. And I should be as big as a house by then. Thanks for that." I walk up to my brother and soon to be sister and give them both a big hug. Another wedding soon!

"To Austin and Leah finally setting a wedding date." Dad proudly toasts. You hear everyone clinking their glasses and cheering.

****

"Karlie and Leah, can I talk to you two for a second?"

"Sure Maysen, what's up? Everything okay?" Karlie asks.

"I just wanted to take an extra minute to thank you two for all you did to get Audrey and I back together. Thank you for accompanying her to Omaha even if it was a wasted trip. Thank you for helping her get the courage to tell me about the baby. Without you two I'm not sure we would be standing here right now and I wouldn't have this ring on my left hand. And most of all I want to thank you for that little outfit you picked out for Audrey for our date in Omaha. That was the most amazing thing I had ever seen."

"Was?" Leah asks not sure she's happy with that answer.

"Until I saw her coming down the aisle towards me tonight.

She looked like an angel that God sent down just for me."

"You two deserve to be happy. Fate was working overtime for you two. Just be happy and love Audrey with all you are." They each give me a quick hug and walk away to the love of their lives. Love sure is big on this ranch. I am so happy and proud to be in the middle of it now too.

****

"Tracey, I am so glad you could be here tonight. But how in the world did you get here so quickly?"

"I wondered when that question was coming. I hadn't left town yet. I only told you I did because I could tell how much you and Prince Charming wanted to be alone. Then when I got to my hotel room Carter came and knocked on the door."

"I'm going to kill him. He didn't hurt you did he?"

"Of course not! He and I have been hanging out and talking. He is a really messed up guy. He's got some issues he needs to deal with and I've been trying to help him through it. That is what I do for a living now you know!"

"Oh whew, I thought I was going to have to go from wedding to jail in an hour." I laugh and give her a big hug.

"No we're good. I wouldn't have missed this for the world though. You look so beautiful and happy."

"Thank you for being here. You mean the world to me."

"Ditto. I need to get back but I will talk to you soon. Love you so much."

27

"Congratulations Maysen. It was very beautiful. Very happy for you two of you. She's a wonderful girl but we all know I think that because I tried setting you up with her a while back." Uncle Sam says after I say goodbye to Carter.

"It was the best day of my life. Thank you for coming. We appreciate it with the short notice and all."

"It was no bother. We were glad we were able to be here. Your Aunt got tired of being gone from home and was worried sick about you Mama. We were already almost home when she got ahold of us. Gave us a good reason to get all spiffed up."

"Mom has missed Aunt Ingrid too. I wasn't enough company for her."

"I wanted to talk to you about the garage. How's it been going?"

"Great. Nothing out of the ordinary I don't think."

"Well, have you made up your mind about buying it?"

"Actually I have. I think it's time we sat down and

hammered out the details. Price, timeline, etc."

"No need. The place is all yours. I'll have my lawyer work up the papers and it'll be a done deal. Wedding and baby present from your Aunt and me."

"Oh Uncle Sam that's too much."

"No it's not. It's perfect for me. I don't need the money and I don't need the garage either. You change the name to whatever you want it to be and it will be yours. Your new family will do it justice too with any new ideas you can come with. It's a tired old place but it works until you're ready to go bigger."

"Uncle Sam I don't know what to say. Thank you so much." I give the old man a hug and hold on for a few extra seconds. This is the only way I know to get him to understand just how much this means to me."

"You are more than welcome and I should be thanking you for allowing me to retire. I've been enjoying it and so has your Aunt. I'm always here if you need anything. Which I'm sure you won't though. Good luck in the business and your new life. You're a good man and I'm proud to hand my business over to you."

"Thank you. I'm going to go find my bride now." We shake hands and I can't wait to tell Audrey all about this new development. This day keeps going and going. My head's spinning with all that's happened. Now, where is my angel?

****

"You look so beautiful Audrey. I can't imagine you looking more radiant than you did when you walked down that aisle towards me. I thought my heart was going to pound out of my chest." I hear Maysen say later that evening after the festivities started to wind down. I'm starting to drag and needed to sit down. I walked over to Mom's pond in the corner of the yard where I always used to sit and read when I was growing up.

THIRD TIME'S A CHARM

I look up at him and can't quit smiling. He's my husband. Forever. All mine.

"Everything looked so perfect. Mom and I used to sit around at bedtime and dream up what my wedding would be like someday. I had forgotten but obviously my mother never did. It looks exactly like we had planned. You were so handsome up there Maysen." I kiss him when he sits next to me on the bench.

"She loves you honey. Of course she remembered. You're only going to get married once you know." And he pulls me closer to kiss my temple at that moment. The love that flows in my veins right now is so intoxicating that I am feeling light headed. I rest my head on Maysen's shoulder and sigh.

"This really is our life now. I'm so happy Maysen."

"Me too. Are you about ready to go home? Um, we haven't even talked about where home's going to be. Where do you want to live?"

"I want to rent Austin's house until we can build our own out here on the ranch like Aiden and Karlie did. What do you think about that?" I look up at Maysen praying he's good with that plan.

"I am perfectly okay with that plan. I was actually going to suggest it just now. Let's go home then. I want to show you just how much I love you. I want to show my wife how much I love her. All night long if she can stay awake."

"I will try. You'll just have to work extra hard to keep me awake handsome."

"Is that a challenge Audrey Correli?" I smile the biggest smile ever as I hear my name said from his lips.

"I love the sound of that. Say it again."

"Audrey Correli. Audrey Correli." He pulls me onto his lap and kisses me with wild abandon. This is going to be the most exciting life anyone could ever lead.

28

"You were right, third time was the charm for those two Amelia." AJ says to Amelia form across the yard where they are watching their daughter and new son be so happily in love.

"Now if we could just get that oldest son of yours married too. He's the tough one." Amelia says to AJ. "He's a lot like his father. Strong, loyal, driven, and very stubborn."

"You got through to me, I'm sure a woman can do that to him one day. It's a shame he had to miss his sister's wedding but there's no way he could make it home in time from wherever he is tonight. Some construction site somewhere I'm sure." AJ says and pulls Amelia's hand into his and kisses her knuckles.

"That's easier said than done. Trust me."

"Maybe so, but where do you think our children got their determination and love for life from? You, my dear. You have shown them what life is about and they live every day just like you taught them."

"Where did I go so wrong with Aaron? He doesn't even want to be around the ranch, let alone Colvin. He hasn't been home since Aiden and Karlie's wedding."

"I know honey. I'll call him tonight after everyone goes home and see what he's up to."

"I have tried to call him at least once a day every day of the week. He's never available and never calls me back."

"He's busy making something of himself on his own honey. He wants to do it alone and without the Blake name getting him there. He's the most stubborn one yes, but he's also the most driven."

"He should slow down some. He's almost forty years old and doesn't have a family. I worry about him."

"You can worry all you want but it's not going to change anything."

"I know." She lays her head on AJ's shoulder and sighs.

"Three out of four isn't bad. You have another wedding to start planning. You'll have a little more time with the next one." He snickers.

"Thank goodness! I'm not sure I could pull this off again if I tried. Audrey always wanted exactly what you see here. Even when she was a child, she always knew she wanted a family of her own. I'm so happy she found that."

"Sam told me he gifted the garage to Maysen. It's all his. That should make you happy too."

"She'll have ties to keep her here too. Wonderful. Let's go start shooing people away. I am exhausted." She stands and reaches for AJ once he stands up too. They embrace and both smile knowing their children are happy tonight. Well, most of them are.

Epilogue

Two months later

"Leah Dawn, I give you this ring, wear it with love and joy. I choose you to be my wife, to have and to hold from this day forward for better or for worse, for richer for poorer, in sickness and in health, to love and to cherish as long as we both shall live."

"Austin William, I give you this ring, wear it with love and joy. I choose you to be my husband, to have and to hold from this day forward for better or for worse, for richer for poorer, in sickness and in health, to love and to cherish as long as we both shall live."

"By the power vested in me, I now pronounce you husband and wife. Austin, please kiss your bride." Reverend Lowell instructs with a wide grin.

Austin envelopes Leah in his arms and they kiss for what seemed like an eternity. I'm not sure if anyone even knows I'm here but the wedding of my other little brother won't be all that's celebrated tonight. I see the newlywed couple walk down the aisle and before Austin can catch sight of me; I duck behind the last row of chairs. Now isn't the time. This should be all about Austin and Leah. Even though a wedding is nothing but a waste of time and hard earned money, if you ask me anyway.

I didn't make it home for my little sister's wedding because I was stuck in Chicago brokering a very large job for my company. The new airport their building will bring in more money than I have brokered yet and I am in desperate need of it.

"Well, if it isn't the lost sheep that found his way back to the flock!" I hear a familiar male voice from behind me. Dad.

"Hi there. Didn't think I would miss another happy ever after did you?" I take the big hug Dad was offering. It does feel great to see everyone again. Even if it's just for the night.

"Your Mama was pretty worried when you didn't respond to the invite or any phone calls."

"I know. Things have been so busy I'm not sure which direction I'm going."

"Just glad to see you here. She's going to be ecstatic when she's your handsome face. Wow son, that handsome face looks tired. Do you ever relax?"

"Not much time for that Dad. Where's Mom at? I better go say hello." I walk away feeling as if I dodged a big bullet there. I can't even begin to tell my family where I've been or what I've been through lately. They wouldn't approve and I wouldn't want to see the disappointment on their faces. Dad's especially.

"Hey beautiful. How about a hug for a weary traveler?" I say from behind my mother hoping those she's talking to don't give me away.

She turns around and has the most angelic look of happiness on her face. "Aaron! I am so glad to see you! When did you get in? We weren't sure you were going to make it. I'm so so glad you did."

We stand there in front of all the wedding guests hugging a few seconds longer than were needed. I have missed her most of all. She's such a ray of light and happiness. I have definitely needed a lot more of that in the past couple of years.

"You look so tired honey. Have you slept at all since the last time I saw you?" She runs her hand along my cheek and frowns with concern.

"I'm just a little jet lagged Ma. No big deal. The wedding was great. They look just as happy as Aiden and Karlie did on their wedding day."

"And Audrey on hers. Have you seen her and Maysen yet? She's going to be so happy to see you too. And your brothers."

"I'll see them all in due time Ma. I'm not going to disappear on you. I'm here."

"For how long son? Audrey's not due for a couple of weeks but she's been having some pretty strong contractions so you might have your first nephew any day now."

"We'll see Ma." No need to upset her now. She'll be just that when she finds out that I'm leaving again in the morning.

"Let's go see your father. Have you seen him yet?"

"Yes, he's the one who told me where you were."

"Well, we have to get things ready for the reception in the equipment barn out at the 6AB. Daddy moved all the equipment out and we had the place all prettied up for Leah and Austin. They wanted rustic so to keep away from the smell of manure, the equipment barn was the only place big enough that would work. I could really use your strong arms."

"Let's go then." Mom and I head out the back of the church and to my rental car.

****

"We need to get the flowers out on those tables before Amelia shows up and panics. That head table looks plain without them. She specifically asked for at least the tables to be done before she got here after the ceremony." Amie directs her forty workers. Being an event planner for a large wedding like this is a dream come true. No one gets this type of opportunity without first having to serve under those who don't care about their workers. "Once those arrangements are on there, we'll be right on time. She should be here any moment too."

"It looks so amazing Amie! I love it and Leah's going to be blown away by how you've transformed this old barn into something so beautiful. It's exactly what they envisioned. You're a miracle worker!" Amelia screams in excitement when she walks in the side door of the barn.

"Everything looks okay? They're headed out now to get the arrangements on the tables. I take it the ceremony is over and the rest of the crowd will be coming soon? They're about ready with all the food and drink too. Champagne and sparkling cider."

"Perfect. I'm going to keep you in mind for the next Blake wedding." Amelia beams then looks at the gentleman next to her and her smile fades just as quickly. Who is this guy that can make her smile turn to a frown so quickly?

"Everything okay Amelia? Is this gentleman bothering you?" I ask stepping forward.

"Oh no don't be silly. This is my oldest son Aaron. I was just trying not to ask him what I always ask him."

"When are you going to find the right woman and settle down Aaron?" The gentleman mocks with a smile on his face now.

"Oh son you know I have your best interests at heart."

"Yes I do. That's the only reason I keep answering you the same way. I don't have time for a woman let alone a marriage." He kisses his mother on the forehead and storms off. Touchy subject I take it.

"Sorry about that. Don't mind him. He's just gotten in from Chicago or Denver. I'm not sure which it is this time. Remind me to introduce you later. You would be a wonderful wife with your organizational skills."

"Oh no. I have a boyfriend. One is enough thank you. Are you ready for the herd of people to enter? Do things look right to you?" I ask trying to change the subject. I don't want to explain to Amelia why I don't want a man in my life. It's much easier to say I have a boyfriend; people tend to leave you alone when they think you're already taken.

"Well dear, if that changes, you let me know. I would love to introduce you to Aaron. He needs someone sweet and light in his heavy and busy life."

****

Does she always think she needs to set me up? This family thinks of nothing other than happily ever after. Fairy tales are for little girls.

I think I've snuck out before anyone can see me just as I hear, "So he is alive?"

"Aiden. How are you? Austin sure looked happy didn't he? Never thought he'd be the one to snag the model."

"I'm sure you've had your fair share of models brother. How the heck are ya?"

"Not too bad. Just tired from the flight. How are you?"

"Great. Tired from the little girl that doesn't like to sleep very much at night. Besides that I'm great."

"Good to hear. What's new with you?"

"Not much really. The breeding program has taken off and it's going great. Got us a new foreman that's working out even better than we thought. Not the same without Gene but things are a new normal with Jason."

"Good to hear. Look I need to go get my stuff inside and shower before too much of this party starts. I'll catch you when I get back. Tell Karlie to save me a dance." I wink at my brother and walk towards the house. I can't wait to get inside the four walls that have been the only place that's felt like home since I was a little boy.

"Where you running off to? Ditching your Mom already?" I hear from behind me just as I get inside the kitchen door.

"I'm sorry I never got your name. What the hell are you doing in my parents' kitchen? Party guests are supposed to be out there."

"I'm the event planner you moron. I had to come up here and get another case of champagne before everyone got there. What are you doing in here and not out there? This is a joyous time for your family."

"Yes it is but I need to shower and decompress. Been a long week and an even longer flight."

"Well, I'll leave you to it and get back down there. My name is Amie Benjamin by the way."

"Aaron. Blake obviously." I crack a hint of a smile as she does the same. I'm not sure who this girl is but she's different than any of the girls I've met over the years. She reminds me of my sister. Speaking of sister, I had better get in gear and get back out there. Everyone's going to know I was here and wonder where I went and send the search party after me.

****

That guy's got one chip on his shoulder goodness. He acted like I was there to rob his family or something. I thought I was past all of that.

I head back towards the party and smile when I hear the laughter coming from within the big barn. I honestly wasn't sure I could pull off turning this nasty old barn into a beautiful spot for a rustic wedding reception. Especially for a famous model. I used to want to be just like her before I figured out I wanted to plan parties. Leah had it all. Money, fame, handsome husband and then she just vanished. No one really knew why she was gone until her tell all interview came out. That was heartbreaking and from that moment on I decided maybe the spotlight wasn't what I wanted.

Walking in the back door I see that everyone has gathered around the food table and ready to eat. "There are a lot of hungry people out there. Are you all ready for this? Put your game faces on and let's do this." I usher the first tray of food out and until the last one has come back empty, I don't stop.

"That's it folks. I want to thank you so much for your help today. Once the guests are all finished eating you can start clearing their plates. Then we can get back here cleaned up and you can go on to your hotel rooms."

I don't normally have enough of a staff to do such a big even so I had to hire people to come down from Tulsa to help. Paying them extra was a little rough on the bottom dollar but it was needed for this size of a party. If we pull this one off without a hitch, maybe Amelia will tell her friends and we'll get hired again. Wouldn't that be great? Sleeping in my car is getting old. I would love to be able to rent a house or apartment. That's a long way in the future though. My old car needs some major work done to it before I can move on. Hopefully this job today will get me enough publicity that I don't have to move on. I would really like to find a nice place to call home again.

"Amie, you did such an amazing job! Thank you. I will be recommending you to everyone I know." Amelia says and hugs me after the bulk of the work's been done.

"We're almost all cleaned up and then the workers will go back to town. Is there anything else you might need?"

"No dear, but I would like you to come and meet my

family."

"Okay but are you sure that's proper? I am just the hired help"

"Oh goodness you're more than that! Come meet them all!"

****

"MAYSEN! Oh my goodness Maysen it's time. The baby's coming. Oh my, the baby is coming!" We hear Audrey scream from across the room where she's standing with Leah and Karlie. She's looking down at her feet and we see a puddle underneath her. That baby is coming right now.

"Come on Audrey. Maysen. I'll get you to the clinic. Can you hang on that long?" I ask my little sister as she begins to panic. I'm not sure she's ready to have this baby yet. She looks so young and pretty tonight and I can't wrap my head around her about to have a baby. That's unreal.

"Yes, please hurry. Honey we came with Leah so I think it's best to have Aaron take us. Don't you?"

"Of course. Let's go. I don't care how we get there; I just want to get there. Our son can't be born in a barn!" Maysen yells, picks up Audrey and hurries to my rental car. This just might be a stain they want to charge me for. I shrug and get inside ready for our quick trip to town.

"We'll be fine Aud just breathe like they taught you in Lamaze."

"What the hell do you know about Lamaze Aaron?" She cusses at me. She really is freaked out if she's cussing at me. I smile thinking back to when she was four and we tried teaching her to say cuss words. Boy did we get a whooping for that!

"Whatever you're smiling about you better stop and get me to a doctor!"